Overload!

"Terry," a breathy voice called. It was Jazz, who was walking over to them. "Have you seen Kim? Oscar's looking for her."

"Who's this Oscar kid?" Jace asked suspiciously. "And why's he looking for you, Kim?"

"Ummm . . ." Kim began helplessly. She felt like a cornered animal.

"There she is, Oscar," Crystal's voice announced happily. "I knew she was here somewhere."

This is not really happening, Kim thought helplessly as five pairs of eyes stared at her. Her life was about to end — all because she'd said yes to too many people. She felt terrible that she hadn't confided in her friends, who might have been able to help her out. She hadn't even been able to tell Breezy since she wasn't talking to her.

And now she had two dates to the same dance and a big game to *pitch* the next day. What was she going to do?

THE PINK PARROTS

CHANGE-UP

Created By Lucy Ellis

By E. J. Valentine

A *SPORTS ILLUSTRATED FOR KIDS* BOOK

First Edition

Library of Congress Cataloging-in-Publication Data
Valentine, E.J.
    Change up / by E.J. Valentine ; created by Lucy Ellis ; [interior line-art by Jane Davila].
        p.   cm.—(The Pink parrots ; #5)
    "A Sports illustrated for kids book."
    ISBN 0-316-74113-2
    [The Pink Parrots run into trouble when their captain Breezy Hawk is injured and shortstop Kim Yardley must take over under Breezy's critical eye. 2. Baseball—Fiction. 3. Friendship—Fiction.] I. Title. II. Series.
pZ7.V2337Ch   1991
[Fic]—dc20   91-14763

For further information regarding this title, write to Little, Brown and Company, 34 Beacon Street, Boston, MA 02108

Published simultaneously in Canada by Little, Brown & Company (Canada) Limited

Created by Lucy Ellis
Written by E.J. Valentine
Cover art by Michael Garland
Interior line art by Jane Davila
Produced by Angel Entertainment, Inc.

1

"You can do it, Betsy!" shouted Amy "Breezy" Hawk, captain of the Pink Parrots, from the on-deck circle in front of the Parrots dugout.

"Send it to the moon!" echoed Kim Yardley, the Parrots shortstop and Breezy's best friend. Standing right behind the dugout fence, Kim anxiously pulled on one of her red braids and stared at Betsy Winston, the Parrots leftfielder, who tightened her grip on the bat. Kim was itching to get to bat, but she wasn't due up for a while. It was the bottom of the sixth and the Pink Parrots, the only all-girls team in the Eastern Maryland Baseball League (called Emblem), were down by two, 9-7, against Ten Pin Bowling. There were two outs. Kim wanted to get in there and bring the Parrots back into the game. She loved a challenge.

Kim watched as Chris Lavery, who was Ten Pin Bowling's star reliever, as well as one of the best pitchers in Emblem, went into his windup. His fastball rocketed over the plate, and Betsy barely got her bat around before

1

the ball thumped into the catcher's mitt.

"Strike one!" the umpire announced.

Breezy groaned and hit the dirt with her bat. "We spent all that time last week on fastballs, and look what happens," she said, turning to Kim. "She gets one fastball and she acts like she's never seen anything like it before."

"Well, Breeze," Kim replied philosophically, "that ball was fast — so fast it almost deserved a speeding ticket."

"Very funny, Shorty," commented Terry DiSunno, the Parrots catcher. She moved to stand next to Kim at the dugout fence.

The shortest girl on the team and one of the shortest in the entire seventh grade at Eleanor Roosevelt Junior High, Kim had been called Shorty on and off practically forever. But it didn't bother her at all. Everyone in her family was short — both her parents and all six kids, although Ryan, the baby, wasn't a year old yet so it was hard to tell if he would be short, too.

"I don't know how you can joke around when we're letting these musclehead jocks from Ten Pin Bowling walk all over us," Terry continued.

"Muscleheads?" Kim questioned, trying to hide her smile. It was so hard for her to look serious. "Don't you mean pinheads, Ter?"

"What are you, a comic?" Terry said, smiling in spite of herself as she tucked a loose strand of dark hair behind her ear.

"Why are they pinheads?" a breathy voice asked from behind Kim and Terry. "Do they have little tiny heads, or something? Or, are they wearing special pins on their hats?"

"Jazz!" Breezy exploded, turning around to face her cousin. "Will you get a grip and pay attention to the game?"

"I *am* paying attention," retorted Jasmine Jaffe, the Parrots rightfielder, with her hands on her hips and her blue eyes sparkling defiantly. She tossed her long blonde hair over her shoulder for emphasis and glared at Breezy.

"Come on, Betsy!" Kim cut in, focusing the girls' attention back on the field. Kim couldn't believe how much Jazz and Breezy bickered sometimes. They were first cousins, after all — even if they were complete opposites in just about everything.

Kim forgot about both of them as she watched Betsy swing wildly at Chris's next pitch. Her bat wasn't even level.

"Strike two!" the umpire called.

"Geesh!" Breezy exclaimed in frustration, shaking her head fiercely so that her dark-blonde ponytail swung from side to side. "Concentrate, Betsy! You can do it!" she yelled.

Kim watched Betsy stare at her cleats for a long minute without moving. Betsy was one of those hit-or-miss hitters. Sometimes she was really on and could get things going, but sometimes she couldn't connect with even the most perfect pitches. Kim could understand why Breezy sometimes got upset at Betsy's hitting. Consistency is important in baseball.

Shrugging, Kim crossed her fingers and stared intently at Betsy. Besty straightened her shoulders and dug her back foot into the dirt in the batter's box.

"You know, Ten Pin Bowling has the cutest lineup of any team in Emblem," Jazz commented, pulling a hot-pink comb out of the back pocket of her uniform and running it through her hair. "Don't you think so, Kim?"

"I don't know," Kim replied. "Hammerin' Hank on Burger Bonanza is pretty hot if you ask me."

"What?!" Jazz asked, sounding totally surprised. "Hammerin' Hank is almost bald and he's so big and dorky looking, he looks like . . . like . . . a human dinosaur. Yuck!"

"Jazz, Hammerin' Hank has a crew cut," Kim said, grinning. "By no stretch of the imagination is the kid going bald."

"Yeah, Jazz," Terry agreed, smiling at her best friend. "I mean, twelve is a little young to go bald. Now pay attention to the game."

"Let me finish," Jazz insisted. "Think about it. Chris Lavery is really cute, John Connelly is really, really cute, and Matt Ryan is gorgeous. But the absolutely cutest one of all on the whole entire team is the catcher, Jace Jeffries. And isn't that the most romantic name?"

"Jazz, how could you even see what he looks like from your position in rightfield?" Kim pointed out logically, her brown eyes twinkling with amusement. She couldn't believe how boy-crazy Jazz was sometimes. It was totally unbelievable.

"He's in my math class," Jazz replied seriously. "And he is to die for. Totally."

Suddenly, the crack of the bat hitting the ball interrupted their conversation. Kim turned quickly to scan the field, a little ticked that she had missed something. A line drive was whizzing between the first and second basemen. Even Jazz stopped talking. The Parrots watched Betsy freeze at the plate, bat in hand, a shocked expression on her face.

"Run!" Breezy yelled, trying to stir Betsy into action.

It worked. Betsy dropped her bat and took off for first base. She beat the rightfielder's throw by a mile.

"Way to go, Betsy!" Kim shouted, a big grin stretching across her freckled face. Great, she thought. The Parrots had a runner on first and the top of the order was coming up. She'd be sweating if she was on Ten Pin's team. Two runs were not enough insurance against the Parrots, that was for sure. Besides a challenge, the thing Kim loved best about baseball was a good comeback.

Breezy gave Kim the thumbs-up sign as she trotted out to the plate.

"Bring Betsy home, Breezy!" yelled Ro, the Parrots coach, as she walked toward the dugout. Kim had to smile at Rose Ann DiMona, their coach. The owner of the Pink Parrot Beauty Salon, the official sponsor of the team, Ro had two major loves in life: baseball and beauty. And she was really good at both. Kim thought Ro was the best coach in Emblem, even if she did dress sort of strangely. Today, for instance, she had on a pair of bright yellow baggies with hot-pink weightlifters marching all over them, and the pants were so baggy, Kim thought they brought new definition to the term. She was also wearing a pink and yellow striped leotard underneath her Pink Parrots jersey.

"You can get those runs back, no problem!" Ro added, blowing a big bubble with her pink bubblegum.

"Show these pinheads what we're made of, Breeze!" Kim shouted as Breezy took a few practice swings. "Don't spare 'em!"

Terry groaned and nudged Kim with her elbow. "You and the bowling cracks," she commented, pretending to frown. "You're too much, Shorty. I can't take it."

"Can't take what?" Jazz asked.

"Never mind," Terry said without turning around.

"Hey, Kim," Jazz began, "do you want me to rebraid your hair since you're up soon?"

"No thanks, Jazz," Kim replied, her gaze focused on Breezy, who had crouched into her low stance at the plate. "Anyway, it's only going to get more messed up when I put on my batting helmet."

"But Kim, you're going to be within inches of Jace

6

Jeffries and I'm telling you, I know you're going to want to look your best," Jazz asserted solemnly.

"Check it out," Kim said, changing the subject, as the entire Ten Pin infield and outfield took a few steps backward. "Breezy's up to something. Look at those dudes back up."

"Psych!" Terry yelled, banging the fence with her hand. "How she gets them to fall for it every time, I'll never know."

"You know Breezy's one of the greatest at playing head games," Kim replied. She had to admit, however, that it was incredible that Breezy had played this same head game with every team in the league, and they always bought it. She acted as if she was swinging for the fences, and everyone backed up. Then, she placed a soft little bunt in front of home plate and caught them all off-guard. It was quite a talent. Kim had tried it once, but she couldn't keep a straight face and started cracking up as soon as the infielders stepped back.

Kim watched Breezy step into Chris's first pitch and place a very gentle bunt a few feet in front of the catcher. Kim whistled in admiration as the Ten Pin catcher, Jace Whatever-His-Face, dived after the ball. Breezy easily beat out the throw to first. Then she waved a triumphant fist at Kim, as the first baseman threw his hat down in disgust. Breezy was definitely the master of the bunt — no doubt about it.

"Send it out of here, C.J.!" Kim yelled as Crystal

Joseph, the tall and graceful Parrots first baseman, set up in her picture-perfect batting stance at the plate. A talented ballerina, C.J. had surprised Kim and Breezy by turning out to be a natural baseball player. She hadn't known a single thing about baseball when she had signed up for the team, but she'd learned how to play by reading a ton of library books on the sport. Now, she was one of the most consistent players on the Parrots — consistently good.

Kim knew that Breezy thought learning baseball that way was the weirdest thing she'd ever seen, but it made sense to Kim. That was how she had learned everything about science. You had to read all the background information on whatever experiment you were conducting before you could do it and really understand what you were doing. Just doing it wasn't enough. You had to be able to interpret the results.

Kim picked up her special blue aluminum bat. It was smaller and lighter than the Parrots' other ones and suited Kim perfectly. Kim headed out of the dugout toward the on-deck circle, swinging the bat by her side.

Kim watched as Crystal took Chris's first pitch for a ball.

"Good eye, Crystal!" Kim called out. "A walk's as good as a hit!"

Getting the ball back, Chris took off his cap, ran his fingers through his auburn hair, and then jammed his cap back on. He didn't throw too many balls and was obviously a bit put-out that he had thrown one to Crystal — and as tall as she was, she had a big strike zone. Chris fired the next pitch right up the center of the plate.

"Stee-rike one!" the umpire called.

"He is so gorgeous!" Kim heard Jazz exclaim from behind her. She didn't turn around. While Kim could not imagine being as incredibly boy-crazy as Jazz was, it didn't bug her the way it bugged Breezy. Meanwhile, Kim wondered which guy Jazz was referring to — Chris, Matt, Jace. Knowing Jazz, she probably meant all of them.

Chris went into his windup and delivered a bullet, disguised as a baseball. Kim held her breath as Crystal brought her bat around in a smooth, even arc while shifting her weight forward. With a loud *thwack*, Crystal's bat connected with the ball and sent it flying out to the gap between the leftfielder and centerfielder. Crystal dropped her bat, put her head down, and sprinted for first. Breezy was already rounding second as Betsy reached third. Kim saw Andrea Campbell, their third baseman who was acting as third-base coach this inning, give Betsy the signal to keep going. Betsy headed home and Breezy charged toward third. Crystal had held up at second, notching a nifty double, and Andrea was frantically signaling to Breezy to hold up at third.

But Kim could tell Breezy wasn't even looking at Andrea. She knew the only thing on Breezy's mind was scoring the tying run. Nothing was going to stop her.

Kim had seen that expression on Breezy's face many times. It was her "run over people" face. Breezy was going to score — and that was that. Kim was glad she wasn't Ten Pin's catcher. Things were going to be ugly.

"Come on, Breezy!" Kim yelled, her red braids bobbing as she jumped up and down in excitement. "Tie up the game!"

She saw John Connelly, Ten Pin's third baseman, snag the cutoff throw, pivot, and rifle the ball toward home. Kim glanced at Breezy digging for home plate. She knew it was going to be close — very close.

"Slide, Breezy, slide!" Ro yelled from the dugout.

Suddenly, everything seemed to be happening in slow motion. The sounds of the screaming crowd faded away. Breezy's face was frozen into a grimace of concentration, her cap was halfway off her head, and her steps seemed to be keeping time with the pounding of Kim's heart. Kim didn't even breathe as, inch by inch, the ball got closer to the catcher's waiting mitt and Breezy got closer to the plate and to scoring the tying run.

Then Breezy dropped to the ground in a textbook hook slide as the ball thumped into the catcher's mitt. Since it wasn't a force play, Jace was going to have to make the tag. Kim closed her eyes. She couldn't stand to watch.

"Safe!" she heard the umpire bark out.

The entire Parrots dugout erupted in cheers. Kim sighed loudly with relief and opened her eyes.

"What's the matter with Breezy?" Jazz asked a moment later. "Why isn't she getting up?"

Kim was wondering the same thing. She didn't even stop to answer Jazz, but zipped out of the dugout and over to home plate.

Breezy was lying on the plate, holding her left knee, and rocking back and forth. Kim could tell she was in major pain. She could also see that Breezy was biting her lip so she wouldn't cry. Kim knew that Breezy would do almost anything before she would ever cry or lose control in public. In fact, in all the years Kim had known Breezy, she had seen her cry only once, and she had not cried since. It happened when they were 6 years old. Breezy's brothers had played baseball with all the boys in the neighborhood. Breezy and Kim had wanted to play more than anything, but the boys wouldn't let them. Breezy had starting crying and Kim remembered Tom, Breezy's oldest brother, telling her, "See, all girls do is cry. We don't want you on our team." So she and Kim had begun practicing baseball nearly six hours a day. The next summer, Tom and the rest of the boys had almost begged Breezy and Kim to join their team.

"Hey, Breeze," Kim said, as she reached her friend, "are you all right? That was almost a *Guiness Book of World Records* slide. You really tore up the base path. I could see the sparks flying all the way from the on-deck circle. You were hot." She giggled, hoping that Breezy wasn't hurt badly, and not knowing what else to say.

Breezy cracked a smile, and Kim sighed in relief. She couldn't be hurt too badly if she was smiling.

"Are you all right, hon?" Ro suddenly asked. Kim looked up, surprised to see that a crowd had gathered around home plate. "Can you stand up? Can we help?"

"Don't move her!" Crystal cried out. "I was just reading something about accident victims. You shouldn't move them unless you determine the extent of injuries first, and you need a trained paramedic for that."

"You were reading a book on accident victims?" Kim asked in shock. She knew Crystal read a lot of books, but accident victims seemed like a bizarre topic.

"Guys . . ." Breezy said softly.

"It was on CPR," Crystal explained.

"Guys . . ." Breezy repeated.

"Well, maybe we should get some trained paramedics, then," Terry said, elbowing her way to the front of the crowd. "And where are her parents?"

"Hey —" Breezy began yet again.

"Over at Field Three," Kim replied, cutting Breezy off. She pointed toward one of the other fields in the park. "They're watching part of Danny's game."

"I'll go get them," Crystal offered, breaking into a run as soon as she cleared the group of people huddled by home plate.

"Somebody go call the paramedics!" Terry added.

"There's an ambulance stationed by the park office," Ro said. "Jazz, go tell them to bring a stretcher, okay?"

Breezy closed her eyes and groaned.

"Breeze, are you all right?" Kim asked in concern.

"I don't need a stretcher," Breezy complained, turning to glare at Kim. "I'm not a wimp."

"Well, can you stand up?" Kim asked logically, not put off by Breezy's grumpy look.

Breezy tried to stand up. She was half-crouched, half-sitting, when she yelped and abruptly sat back down, her left leg stuck out in front of her. "My knee is killing me!"

"Then you need a stretcher," Ro said matter-of-factly. "Go on, Jazz."

Breezy groaned again as Jazz took off.

"Does it hurt that much?" Kim asked, suddenly serious. Breezy didn't sound too good.

"I can't believe you let her send Jazz," Breezy said, moaning. "With my luck, the paramedics will be cute and we won't see Jazz, or them, for a few hours."

Kim giggled as Mr. and Mrs. Hawk suddenly appeared next to their daughter.

"What happened, Amy?" Breezy's mother asked, the concern evident in her voice. "Are you all right?"

"She hurt her knee," Ro explained, not letting Breezy answer. "The paramedics are on the way."

Suddenly, in Kim's mind, everything started to speed up. The paramedics drove the ambulance over to the field, and pushed everyone back. Kim watched as they splinted Breezy's knee and then lifted her onto the stretcher and began to cart her away. Kim stood there

13

staring, frozen in place. She felt very small and helpless all of a sudden.

"Kim!" Breezy called out. "Kim, come here!"

Kim started and ran toward the departing stretcher. "What Breeze? What do you need?"

"The game," Breezy cut in, her dark eyes glittering with determination in her now pale face. "We're all tied up. We have to win. You're up next — it's up to you. Don't let me down. We have to win."

"Will do," Kim said, doing a fake salute. "Anything else, Cap-i-tain?"

Just then Ro put her hand on Kim's shoulder and pulled her back a bit, away from the stretcher.

"Kim! One more thing," Breezy called out, turning her head so that she could face her friend as the stretcher was placed inside the ambulance. "You're the captain while I'm gone, okay?"

"No problem," Kim replied immediately, trying to smile reassuringly at her best friend. "Don't worry about a thing."

Then the emergency guys pushed the stretcher into the back of the ambulance. Mrs. Hawk climbed in with her daughter. The doors were closed with a bang. Kim gulped as she waved good-bye to Breezy. She had this weird lump in her throat. She tried to reassure herself with the thought that Breezy had probably just pulled some little muscle in her knee, or something. She didn't seem to be in that much pain. It was probably no big deal.

People had sports injuries all the time, big important stars like Dave Winfield and Joe Montana. And they got over them. But still, no one on the Parrots had ever been taken away in an ambulance before.

"Are you okay, Kim?" Ro questioned softly, inter-rupting Kim's thoughts.

"Ummm," Kim mumbled, nodding slowly.

Ro put her arm around Kim's skinny shoulders. "Don't worry about Breezy," Ro said gently, squeezing Kim's shoulder. "She's a tough cookie. You know that. Meanwhile, we've got a game to win, and you're up, slugger." Ro smiled, and Kim tried to smile back.

Kim exhaled quickly three times, a trick Terry used to calm down. Terry said she'd gotten it from her mom's shrink, whom her mother had made her see a few times after her parents' divorce.

Ro handed Kim a batting helmet and her bat. She had a game to win. It was now or never, and Kim figured she was about as ready as she ever would be. Anyway, there was nothing she could do to make Breezy better. She shut her eyes tightly for one second and wished that Breezy would be okay. Then she exhaled three times again.

"Send these guys into early retirement!" Kim heard somebody yell. She turned around to see Terry giving her the thumbs-up sign from the dugout. Kim waved back at Terry, and then headed for the batter's box.

"Swing for the stars!" someone yelled and then gig-gled. Kim didn't have to turn around to know it was Jazz.

15

She had her own creative slogans, as well as the most unmistakable giggle.

Kim held up two fingers in a victory salute, and made her way over to home plate.

"So, are you ready to play ball yet, Miss Prima Donna?" an obnoxious voice suddenly asked from right behind Kim. "I mean, I know the rules are different for girls," the voice continued in the same sarcastic tone.

Kim whipped around and found herself face-to-face with the Ten Pin catcher. Well, not exactly face-to-face because he was wearing his catcher's mask so she couldn't see his eyes very well. But his attitude was coming across loud and clear. He hit his hand into his mitt and just stood there.

"What are you talking about?" Kim asked, confused. Didn't she look ready to play, wearing a batting helmet and holding a bat? What was with this guy?

"You heard me, Red," the catcher responded in the same obnoxious voice. "Girls always get off easy. You think you can play a guy's game, but you really can't."

"First of all, my name's not Red," Kim began heatedly. Rarely did she lose her temper, but when she did, she really did. Her dad said she got it from her mother's side of the family. He called it an Irish temper.

"Second of all, the Parrots are living and breathing proof that girls can play baseball just as well as, if not better than, guys, so there," Kim blurted out before she could stop herself. She knew she shouldn't be taking this jerk up on his stupid ideas, but she could not believe he was talking to her like this, especially after Breezy's terrible accident. Being carted off in an ambulance was not her idea of getting off easy.

"Please," the catcher interrupted, pushing his mask up to brush his long dark hair out of eyes, which Kim suddenly noticed were the most unusual shade of light-blue flecked with grey. "You girls only got that run because that girl Breezy hurt herself and the ump felt bad for you because you're girls."

"Listen Lace or Case, or whatever your name is, he didn't give anything to us. Breezy scored a run, fair and square," Kim sputtered, her brown eyes blazing. "So if you don't mind, I have a game to play."

"The name is Jace by the way," Jace replied, coolly eyeing Kim, his jaw working up and down as he chewed a piece of gum. "Just don't talk to me about sportsmanship. Because there is no sportsmanship where girls and sports are concerned. None at all."

"Play ball!" the umpire announced abruptly, interrupting the argument.

Kim whipped around, hoisted her bat, and dug her back foot into the dirt. She had to concentrate. She just had to. Clenching her jaw and narrowing her eyes, Kim eyed the pitcher, visualizing an RBI that would bring Crystal home.

The Parrots were so close to winning, and now that this Jace jerk had said all that junk about girls not being as good as guys, Kim had to show him, show all of them, that not only were girls as good as guys, they were better. And she had to win this game for Breezy, too.

Kim exhaled three times again. She couldn't remember being this mad in a game situation since she and Breezy had quit the Mitchell Lumber team at the beginning of the season because Coach Carpenter wouldn't put the two girls in the lineup.

All right, Breeze, Kim thought to herself as she crouched down into her stance, I'm going to win this one, just like I promised. She gripped the bat even more tightly, and tried not to think about Jace the Jerk who was only inches behind her.

Kim focused her attention on Chris Lavery as he went into his windup. It looked as if the pitch was going to be one of his infamous fastballs. Swinging furiously, Kim realized too late that it wasn't a fastball. Chris's sneaky change-up inched by her moments after she had brought her bat around. Feeling her face flame, Kim didn't think there was anything as embarrassing as being caught swinging because she didn't time a pitch properly.

"Strike one!" the umpire called.

"Good going, Red," Kim heard Jace mutter. But she wouldn't give him the satisfaction of thinking that he had gotten to her by turning around. She had to concentrate and get a hit.

Kim dug in again, and blew her red bangs out of her eyes. This time she wasn't going to fall for any of Chris's tricks. She was going to get a piece of whatever he happened to throw. With her eyes glued to the ball from the moment Chris released it, Kim connected head-on with all of her might. The bat reverberated in her hands as she followed through. She didn't even watch as the ball soared over Chris's head. She ran for first base as fast as she could.

She heard the cheers of the Parrots as she headed on to second. Grinning, she realized then that Crystal must have made it home. The Parrots had won! She couldn't wait to tell Breezy!

2

"Did anybody call me?" Kim blurted out, banging the back door shut, and running into the kitchen.

"Call you what?" asked Richard, her 11-year-old brother, pushing a lock of red hair the same shade as his sister's out of his eyes. "Ugly?"

"Rich, be serious for one second, please," Kim demanded, her hands on her hips as she glared at her brother.

"Okay, serious for one second, take one," he continued, turning the corners of his mouth down and squinting at Kim.

Even Kim had to giggle. "You look like a basset hound when you do that, you know. But I'm serious."

"I'm serious, too," Richard asserted, making his basset hound face again.

"Listen, it's not funny," Kim went on, pacing back and forth in front of the refrigerator.

"Do you hear me laughing?" Richard retorted, pulling the milk carton out of the refrigerator and pouring himself a glass. "You want some milk?"

Kim plopped down on one of the wooden kitchen chairs and shook her head as she stared at her brother, who was leaning against the refrigerator. She took a deep breath.

"What's up, Kim?" Richard asked, pulling himself up onto the counter next to the stove and staring at his sister. "You look kind of sick, like you did that time you ate liver when you thought it was steak."

"Very funny," Kim said, tapping her foot against the yellow and white linoleum floor, and trying not to smile. Her brother was so absurd. And her friends wondered where she got her sense of humor from. Everyone in her family was always making cracks about stuff. They didn't give an inch. It was the Yardley way.

"As you were saying," Richard continued, using his fake James Bond British spy voice. "Hey, who won your game?" he asked suddenly in his normal voice.

"We did," Kim replied. "But —"

"So what do you look sick for?" Richard interrupted. "You are so weird."

"Because Breezy had to get taken to the hospital in an ambulance because she hurt herself sliding into home plate," Kim blurted out in a rush, all the worry hitting her full force all over again.

Just then the phone rang. Kim jumped up and flew around the corner into the hallway. But she was too late. Josh had already picked up the receiver. "Hey, dude,"

Josh said and then giggled, loudly.

Kim rolled her eyes at her 6-year-old brother. He was in this phase where he called everyone dude — even older people, like friends of her parents.

"Josh, let me talk, please," Kim demanded, reaching over to take the phone from her brother.

"I'm on the phone," Josh asserted, perfectly serious.

"Josh, come on," Kim retorted. "I'm not kidding."

"'Bye, dude," Josh said reluctantly into the receiver and then handed the phone to his sister with a frown. "You never let me have any fun." Then he scampered around the corner to the family room.

"Hello," Kim said quickly. "Yardley residence."

"Hey, Kim, so how did we do?" Breezy asked right off the bat.

"How are you?" Kim asked quickly. "How's your knee? Are you okay? Did you get X-rayed? Do you have a cast?"

"Kim, did we win, or didn't we?" Breezy demanded, not answering any of Kim's questions.

"Baseball, baseball, baseball," Kim said, laughing. "You know, you wouldn't get married if your wedding was on the same day as the World Series."

"Wedding? Married?" Breezy asked, sounding confused and impatient. "What are you talking about, Kim? You sound delirious. Did we win or didn't we?"

Kim knew there was no kidding with her best friend when she was like this. Her single-mindedness could sometimes be frightening, Kim thought with a grin. "We won," Kim said quickly. "10-9. I ribbyed Crystal home."

"All right!" Breezy exclaimed. "I would have loved to have seen the look on Chris Lavery's face. He acts like he's the hottest pitcher out of the bullpen since the New York Yankees started using Dave Righetti. Well, before they traded him. I wish I could have been there."

"Me too," Kim agreed. "Now, Breeze, what happened to you? I want all the details. The suspense is killing me."

"I pulled some stupid ligament behind my knee or something," Breezy explained grumpily. "And they're saying I have to stay off it for at least three weeks. But I don't know if I believe them. I can't not play baseball for three whole weeks. I'll go crazy."

"So you're going to play baseball on crutches? Now you know more than doctors?" Kim replied. "Did you go to medical school when I wasn't looking?"

"What are you, my grandmother?" Breezy retorted, sounding angry. "I didn't say I was going to play baseball. I just said I was going to go crazy. All right?"

There was silence for a minute. Kim had known Breezy for too long to be hurt by her tone. She knew that Breezy didn't mean to be obnoxious. She was obviously very frustrated. And this was only the beginning of her injury. It was going to be a very long three weeks.

"Breeze," Kim began, "you could have asked them to rebuild you, you know."

Breezy laughed. "Right. Then I'd be better, stronger,

faster," she said. "It would be unreal."

"So, do you have crutches or are you in a wheelchair?" Kim asked, changing the subject.

"Crutches," Breezy replied. "Can you see me in a wheelchair? I blew all the doctors and nurses away by how fast I could motor down the hall."

"I guess you didn't tell them that you had crutches a couple of years ago when you broke your leg skiing, huh?" Kim retorted with a giggle.

"Well, Kim, they never exactly asked," Breezy said, laughing.

"So, Breeze, what are you supposed to do for your knee?" Kim began seriously.

"Well, ice, of course," Breezy began but Kim couldn't hear the rest because a scream and a loud crash suddenly erupted from the family room.

"Hey, hold on a sec," Kim interrupted Breezy. "I think the dynamic duo just successfully killed each other."

Kim dropped the receiver and went running into the family room. The coffee table was turned on its side in the middle of the rug, and the twins, Josh and Jenny, were sitting all the way over on the other end of the room, looking at it as if it were some kind of wild animal.

"Okay, guys, who did it?" Kim demanded, staring at her youngest brother and sister, and trying to look ferocious. But it was hard not to laugh. They seemed so scared, their blue eyes wide, peeking up at Kim from beneath their identical curly red bangs. Besides, Kim was just not the ferocious type, and the twins knew that.

"Did what?" they echoed in unison — as usual. They did and said stuff in exactly the same way at the exact same time a lot. But Kim was used to it.

"The coffee table," Kim prodded. "You know, the thing that has four legs over there on the rug. The piece of furniture that's usually in front of the couch."

"He did it!" Jenny yelled.

"She did it!" Josh yelled.

"Oh, forget it," Kim admonished with a frown. "I'll deal with you two when I get off the phone. And that's a threat not a promise so don't skip the country, okay?"

"How can we skip the country?" Kim heard Josh ask Jenny as she left the room.

"My legs aren't long enough," Jenny replied.

Laughing, Kim ran back to the hallway and grabbed the phone. "Sorry about that, Breeze," she apologized into the receiver. "Those kids are truly mutant twins. Now, you were saying you had to ice your knee, and what else?"

"Do some stupid exercises and stuff," Breezy replied grumpily. "Maybe even physical therapy. They weren't sure. I have to go back on Monday after school to see the doctor. The swelling better be down by then."

"Oh," Kim said, racking her brains to think of something to cheer Breezy up. Kim didn't like to hear her friend sound so grumpy. Three weeks wasn't a lifetime after all. "Practice won't be the same without you."

"Speaking of practice," Breezy replied. "You should come over to my house tomorrow so we can discuss what I want you to do."

"Okay," Kim said. "And take care of yourself, Hawk. Don't do anything stupid, like one-handed push-ups or anything like that. And no squat thrusts or hamstring curls or dead lifts or —"

"Kim," Breezy quickly interrupted. "I promise not to weightlift — especially since Russ never lets me near his weights anyway."

"Ah, yes, your bodybuilding career has been nipped in the bud by a jealous older brother who's just afraid that you might develop more muscles than Arnold Schwartzenegger."

Breezy giggled. "You are truly warped, Kim."

"What can I say, Arnold?" Kim replied with a giggle, glad to hear Breezy sounding like her old self again. "You're huge. Anyway, I'll see you tomorrow."

"Catch you later!" Breezy said.

As Kim hung up, she heard another crash accompanied by loud barking. She took off around the corner to the family room to see what was up. One of the kitchen chairs was lying next to the coffee table, and both twins and Red, the Yardleys' Irish setter, were lying in front of the TV, quietly watching cartoons.

"Hall right, zee game eez ofer," Kim intoned in her best Dracula voice. "Zee leetle vons must die," she continued as she picked up an afghan off the couch and draped it over her shoulders as if it were a cape.

"Yikes!" Jenny yelped. With a giggle she dove behind the couch.

"I'm not 'fraid of you," Josh said, walking right up to Kim, his freckled face serious. "You're just dumb old Kim."

"Now you're at my mercy," Richard suddenly interrupted, grabbing onto Kim's ankle so that she fell onto the rug with a thump. Before she could move, he twisted one of her arms behind her back.

"Richard," Kim protested. "Let me go."

"Not before my assistants have had their way with you," Richard replied with this phony evil cackle. "Zombie One, Zombie Two, go to it, dudes."

Josh and Jenny giggled delightedly as they pounced on Kim, pulled off her shoes, and began to tickle the bottoms of her feet — her most ticklish spot. Kim was laughing so hard she couldn't even talk, and the tears were running down her face. The next thing she knew, Red had jumped into the action and had started licking her nose.

"Stop!" Kim finally gasped. "Puh-leaze."

"Not until you say the magic words," Richard said, tightening his grip on her arm.

"Yeah, magic words, dude," Josh echoed.

"Yeah," Jenny put in. "Magic words."

Red licked Kim's nose again as if in agreement.

"Hey, I just heard the car," Kim suddenly said.

"Those aren't the magic words," Josh said seriously.

"Yeah, but Mom must be home," Richard added, letting go of Kim. "So it's good enough for now."

"We better clean this place up, pronto," Kim commanded, jumping up and brushing off her uniform pants. Red started to bark and went running toward the back door.

"It's an eleven-bag day," Mrs. Yardley announced from the kitchen. "Let's move it, kids."

"I hate putting groceries away," Richard groaned as he pushed the coffee table back to its original position in front of the couch. "Anyway, it's women's work."

"Listen, you macho chauvinist-type," Kim replied good-naturedly. "I notice that you eat more than anyone else in this house, so you're really the one who should put the groceries away in the first place."

"Yeah, tell me about it," Richard retorted. "You're the one who's always Hoovering the good cookies. I swear those double-stuff Oreos disappear in seconds when you're around."

"Hey, Josh, Jenny, what are you guys doing?" Kim asked, turning to where the two kids were sitting in front of the television.

"Playing Nintendo," Josh answered. "What do you think?"

"Oh, no, you're not, big guy," Kim replied. "You can help with the groceries, too — both of you."

The four kids made their way out to the garage to the

Yardleys' old bottle-green station wagon. Kim gave Josh and Jenny each a small bag of groceries. They weren't exactly the biggest helps, but Kim's parents thought it was important that they learn to pitch in like everybody else. So did Kim. Her father always talked about their family as if it was a team. Actually, what he said reminded Kim of Ro's analogy of the Pink Parrots as spokes on a wheel. Without one spoke, the wheel didn't turn properly. Thinking about the Parrots reminded Kim of Breezy.

"Hey, Ma," Kim said as she plopped three bags down on the kitchen table. "Hey, Ryan, what's up, slugger?" Kim kidded her baby brother, who had been shopping with Mrs. Yardley and was now sitting in his high chair.

"Ma, you will never believe what happened today —" Kim began.

"Oh, Kim, is that all the groceries?" Mrs. Yardley interrupted, smoothing her short blonde hair distractedly with one hand. "I really have to finish getting ready. Remember, my plane leaves first thing in the morning. Can you keep an eye on Ryan while I pack?"

"Oh, yeah," Kim replied, hitting the side of her head with her hand. "How could I have forgotten? You're going to Dallas tomorrow to Aunt Cindy's."

"Oh, and Kim," her mother continued. "We should go over the menu for the week and everybody's schedules. After all, you'll be in charge of the house."

"No problem, Mom," Kim said quickly. "Don't worry

about a thing. I'll have it all under complete and total control."

"Good," Mrs. Yardley replied, the worried expression on her face turning to a smile. "I'm going upstairs to pack then."

"Richie," Kim crooned as soon as her mother had left the kitchen. "Get out here — now!"

"Cool your jets, Kim," Richard mumbled, walking slowly into the kitchen, his head buried in the sports section of the newspaper. Like all of the Yardley family, and many people in their part of Maryland, Richard was a big fan of the Baltimore Orioles. "And don't call me Richie. Hey, listen to this. The Orioles won yesterday, 10-3, and they're talking about upping Cal Ripkin, Junior's salary by at least a million for next year."

"That'll be me one day," Kim said, bending down to put a bagful of apples into the crisper drawer of the refrigerator.

"Yeah, right, Kim," Richard retorted. "Any day now Johnny Oates will sign you up."

"I'm home," a high squeaky voice suddenly announced.

"Is that . . . no . . . could it be . . . the famous Faith Marie Yardley?" Kim asked, turning to face her petite and pretty 10-year-old sister. Kim rarely noticed how people looked, but even she had to admit that Faith was beautiful with her big blue eyes and pale, pale skin. Kim wasn't jealous, though. She and her sister were about as different as two people could possibly be. Faith knew nothing at all about sports or science or anything. She wanted to be an actress and worried about clothes and stuff all the time. Kim sometimes wondered how it was possible that they were even related. She kind of understood how Breezy felt about Jazz. It was hard to believe that the same blood flowed in their veins.

"Here, put this away," Richard said, throwing a loaf of bread in Faith's direction.

Faith missed the bread and it fell with a soft thump to the floor. "Rii-ii-chard," Faith whined, tossing her glossy auburn curls and glaring at her brother. "You'll make me ruin my nails. And my big dress rehearsal is next week, you know."

"How could I forget?" Richard retorted. "You've only been reminding us every day for a month. Now, what is it you're going to be? Head vampire in a horror show? You don't need a costume, right?"

"Shut up!" Faith yelled.

"Stop it, you guys," Kim cut in. "Let's get these groceries put away." There was never a dull moment at their house, Kim thought, sighing.

"Hey, Kim," Faith said, turning to face her sister, a jar of spaghetti sauce in her hand. "Don't forget about my costume. We have to have it finished by Thursday. You promised."

"No problem," Kim said, climbing up onto the counter to put the pasta away in the cupboard above the stove. They should have lower cabinets in this house, she thought, since none of the Yardleys were tall. Her mother kept a stool in the kitchen so she could reach all the top shelves, but Kim found it much easier to hop on a counter than search for the stool every time she needed something. "Now, since Mom's leaving first thing in the morning, I thought for dinner —"

She hopped off the counter to find herself all alone in the kitchen — except for Ryan. He was still sitting happily in his high chair, chewing on some Cheerios. Richard and Faith had disappeared, and Kim could hear Josh and Jenny giggling from the direction of the family room. Shrugging, she filled the spaghetti pot with water.

"So, Ryan, it's just you and me, kid," Kim said. "And tomorrow you get to go on your first big airplane trip. You're just a regular traveling dude, you know. And me? Well, I can handle things, no problem, right?"

Kim walked over to her brother and tousled his hair. Then she picked him up and walked out of the kitchen to go upstairs and see if her mother needed any help.

She'd have to make a list of all the things she had to remember. She'd do it tomorrow before she went to Breezy's and after she helped the kids with T-ball practice. Lists always helped get stuff done. It was so satisfying to cross things off. Besides, she had a ton of stuff to do. But she'd get it all done. She always did.

Kim never let anybody down. No matter what.

3

"Kim, Kim," a voice whispered urgently in Kim's ear on Monday morning at school. She was standing on her tiptoes in front of her locker putting her books away.

"Don't look now," the voice continued in a whisper. "He's only a few feet away from us."

"Who? Why?" Kim retorted immediately. "Is he armed and dangerous, or something, Jazz?"

"Kim, this is serious," Jazz went on, still whispering.

"More serious than a homicidal maniac loose in the halls of Eleanor Roosevelt?" Kim kidded. "I find that hard to believe for some weird reason."

"Kiiiim," Jazz whined in Kim's ear. "I'm serious. Don't even turn around."

"But, Jazz, I have to turn around sometime," Kim pointed out logically, her head still buried in her locker. "I have science class in about two minutes. And I don't think Mr. Krasnow would actually notice or care if I came to his class full of bullet holes, as long as I was on time."

"Oh, no, he's heading right this way," Jazz moaned,

pushing herself closer to Kim. "And I hate these jeans and I didn't wash my hair this morning. I can't believe this. I really can't believe this. Now I know why they're always saying that you should look your best because you never know when you're going to meet your . . . your . . . destiny," Jazz concluded.

"Destiny?" Kim sputtered, finally turning around. She found herself face-to-face with Oscar Slaughterbeck. Jazz was staring pointedly over Kim's shoulder.

"Hey, Oscar. What's up?" Kim asked, grinning at the red-headed boy, who was only a little bit taller than she was.

"Not much," Oscar replied with a smile.

"Jazz," Kim began, turning to where Jazz stood frozen like a statue next to her. "I have one small question. How long have you known that Oscar is your destiny?"

Oscar blushed, and pushed his round gold-rimmed glasses farther up his nose.

"Kim," Jazz hissed, flipping her blonde ponytail over her shoulder. "You know I wasn't talking about Oscar."

"Oh," Kim replied, punching Jazz lightly on the shoulder. "You're making lots of sense now, Jazz."

"Forget it," Jazz suddenly said. "We're safe now. There are so many people in the hallway that if he does see us and we happen to make eye contact with him, it will seem natural, you know. So that's okay," she concluded solemnly.

"Now, I get it," Kim commented, trying not to laugh.

"It's all suddenly clear for me. I have seen the light."

"Oh, my gosh," Jazz suddenly exclaimed. "He's heading right for us. And he's wearing the most to-die-for brown leather bomber jacket. He looks incredible."

"Jazz, who are you talking about?" Kim asked, a note of exasperation in her voice, as she tried to look over the heads of the taller kids in the hallway. Sometimes being short had its drawbacks — like not always being able to see stuff other people could. But on the other hand, sometimes Jazz was just a bit too much to handle with her boy-craziness. "Have you spotted this incredible dude in the animal skin anywhere, Oscar?" Kim asked, nudging Oscar in the ribs.

Just then Jace Jeffries, the Ten Pin Bowling catcher, sauntered up to them, a notebook under one arm and a brown leather jacket slung casually over his shoulder.

"Hey, Red," he said to Kim, staring right into her eyes.

"Who are you talking about?" Kim asked, glaring at him. "There's nobody here by that name." Her *dog* was named Red, for goodness sake.

"Uh . . . hi . . . Jace," Jazz cut in with a toss of her blonde ponytail. "How about that game?" she asked, tossing her hair again. This time, though, Kim wound up with a mouthful of it.

"Ask Red," Jace replied curtly. "I already told her how I felt about the whole thing. Didn't I, Red?"

"Quit calling me Red," Kim exploded, spitting the stray strands of Jazz's ponytail out of her mouth. "My name is Kim. And personally, I don't really care what you think about anything because I think you're a macho chauvinist spoilsport pig!"

"Take it easy, Red," Jace replied casually, eyeing her the same way he had the other day at home plate. "See you around." Straightening the collar of his shirt, he took off down the hall.

"He is incredible!" Jazz exclaimed as soon as he was out of earshot. "He is so, so cool. Why were you so obnoxious to him, Kim? He didn't say anything really obnoxious to you."

At that moment the bell rang and all the seventh-and eighth-graders in the hallway began to rush off to their classes.

"Hey, Oscar, we better hurry," Kim said quickly.

"Yeah, especially since today is D-Day," Oscar said, raising his eyebrows at Kim.

"Oh, yeah, Dissection Day," Kim replied. "Today we get to rip open those poor frogs and take apart their —"

"Ohmygosh!" Jazz suddenly exclaimed.

"Jazz, it's going to be great. It's not such a big deal," Kim explained. "I'm sure you'll be able to handle it — especially since you have Jimmy Hsu as a lab partner. That guy looks like the kind of kid who could really get into dissection."

"No, no, no," Jazz said, her blue eyes wide. "That's not what I meant. I just thought of something a lot more important than a dumb frog."

"A moment of silence, please," Kim said, turning to Oscar. "Jasmine Jaffe has just had an important thought. Since this doesn't happen very often, I think we should pay tribute to it."

"Kim, this is serious," Jazz retorted, her hands on her hips. "Really, really serious. I just realized why Jace was acting like that."

"Because he's a jerk, that's why," Kim replied, hitching up the right strap of her white overalls that always seemed to be falling down. "That was pretty obvious."

"No, no, no," Jazz corrected her immediately. "Jace Jeffries was acting like that because he *likes* you."

"Jazz, you've got to be kidding!" Kim exclaimed. "I think our hatred for each other is pretty mutual. Don't you think so, Oscar?"

"Uh . . . I don't know," Oscar replied, staring down at his sneakers.

"Well, I do," Kim countered. "And now I think we better motor to class or Mr. Krasnow is going to dissect us instead of those frogs."

"Kim, hate and love are just opposites of the same feeling, you know," Jazz continued, running to keep up with Kim as she marched seriously down the hall. "Think of the most famous couples in history. They were always fighting. Like Ted Danson and Kirstie Alley in *Cheers*."

"Jazz, give me a break!" Kim exclaimed. "They were not a famous couple from history, okay?"

"Kim, you don't understand," Jazz continued. "Right, Oscar? Jace couldn't take his eyes off Kim. Right?"

Oscar grunted noncommittally, his eyes glued to his sneakers.

"She's finally lost it, Oscar," Kim said, turning to Oscar. "The thought of frog guts has clearly made her lose her mind. And she hasn't even come near the formaldehyde yet."

"Kim, I know about these things," Jazz went on smugly, tossing her ponytail and hitting Kim in the face with it again. "Mark my words. Jace Jeffries and Kim Yardley are going to be a thing. I'm sure of it."

Kim rolled her eyes at Oscar. "Hey, O, when do you want to start Operation Mice?"

"Pretty soon," Oscar replied quickly. "I mean, we promised Mr. Krasnow we'd have our first results ready to present to him in less than two weeks."

"You guys are so weird," Jazz cut in. "How could you volunteer to do extra credit in science? About mice? Gross!"

"I don't know, Jazz," Kim replied, pretending to be serious. "I guess it's just one of those things. Like the thrill you get when you buy nail polish at the mall. Well, O and I get a thrill out of doing scientific research. I mean, our mice study could be the definitive mice behavioral study of all time."

"Yeah," echoed Oscar with a grin. "The definitive junior-high school study, anyway."

"Kim, I just don't get it," Jazz said seriously. "How could you talk about mice at a time like this? We're talking about love, about what could possibly be the biggest romance of your life!"

"Jazz, let me tell you something that might change your life," Kim retorted, trying to stop herself from cracking up. "Shut up!"

"Very funny," Jazz continued, staring hard at Kim. "Just you wait. I know when something's about to happen between two people. Didn't I tell you about Sean Dunphy and Gwen Billings that time at the mall?"

"Jazz, we all saw him following her around like a puppy dog into all those stupid clothing stores," Kim said. "It didn't exactly take a romance expert like yourself to put two and two together for the rest of us. I mean, Sean Dunphy was never into shopping for girls' clothes before."

"But I knew about it way before then," Jazz interrupted.

Just then, the warning bell rang. Kim shook her head, smiling at Jazz, as the three of them hurried down the hall to class.

4

"Hey, Breeze!" Kim yelled down the hall later that morning. "Wait up!" She trotted over to where her best friend was standing with Peter Tolhurst in front of Breezy's locker. Kim smiled to herself. She wasn't at all surprised to see the two of them together. Breezy would never admit it, but Kim had told Breezy ages ago that she knew that Peter liked Breezy — a lot.

Kim shook her head. She couldn't believe herself. She sounded just like Jazz. Not that she thought Jazz was right about Jace liking her. Anyway, it didn't matter since she thought he was a major macho jerk.

"So, Peter, are you ready for the Parrots to blow you and your auto bodies away this weekend?" Kim asked as she walked up to Breezy and Peter.

"You?" Peter retorted, his green eyes twinkling. "I wouldn't count on it — especially without your pitching sensation here — or should I say, the ruling Queen of Slides."

"Peter!" Breezy yelled, hitting him playfully on the leg with one of her crutches. "No slide jokes please. They're in very poor taste. And never underestimate the power of the Parrots. Kim here is standing in as captain, and you've never experienced her pitching. She can throw bullets that'll knock you out," Breezy added, her face solemn. "Right, Kim?" she asked, turning to wink at Kim.

"Shhh!" Kim said, winking back. "We don't want to give away any of our baseball secrets."

"Of course not," Peter said, looking from one girl to the other and pushing a lock of his curly dark brown hair out of his eyes. "Tricks of the trade, huh? That's what it's all about. Now about these bullets, Kim?"

"Peter!" Kim exclaimed. "Cut it out! You're the enemy. You'll never get it out of me."

"Lunch anyone?" Breezy asked. "I'm starving. Zooming around on these crutches is a real upper-body workout. You know what I'm saying?"

"Oooh!" Kim exclaimed, sticking out her hand to touch Breezy's right bicep. "You are huge."

"Yeah, Breeze," Peter jumped in. "You're so cut, you're cut like a knife just like me," he added, pretending to flex. "Be careful, Kim. You may cut your finger on her muscle."

"All right, you muscleheads," Kim said. "Let's rock and roll."

By the time they got to lunch, the cafeteria was packed. After they'd gone through the line and paid for their food, the three of them stood awkwardly for a minute. Kim didn't know whether Breezy wanted to sit with Peter or not, and Peter didn't seem to be making any moves either way.

It was funny. Breezy was so strong-willed when it came to everything else in the world except for Peter. In a way, Kim thought, it made no sense to her at all. But nothing about romance and dating seemed to follow any sort of scientific logic — if you went by the junk Jazz was always talking about from the tons of magazines she read.

Just then Desmond McGraw, the pitcher for Mel's Auto Body, waved to Peter from a table. Peter said good-bye to the two girls and went over to sit with Desmond. Kim scanned the tables looking for the rest of the Parrots since the team usually sat together at lunch.

"Hey, Shorty, Breeze!" Kim heard somebody yell. "Over here."

Kim saw Terry was waving at them from a table toward the back of the cafeteria. Breezy took off, leaving Kim to carry both of their trays. Following her friend, Kim thought Breezy was doing really well on her crutches, considering how little space there was to maneuver around in.

"You klutz!" Kim suddenly heard a squeaky female

voice exclaim angrily. "Will you watch where you're going?"

"Well, what were your big feet doing out in the middle of the aisle?" Breezy retorted, holding her crutch up as if it were a submachine gun and pointing it right in Lindsay Cunningham's face.

Kim tried not to giggle. Lindsay and Breezy were always going at it. Lindsay considered herself the social queen of their seventh-grade class and she also dated Joey Carpenter, pitcher for Mitchell Lumber. Mitchell Lumber was the team Breezy and Kim had both quit at the beginning of the season because they didn't get enough playing time from the coach, who was Joey's father. There was no love lost between Breezy and Lindsay whatsoever. Lindsay seemed to have a personal vendetta against the Parrots — especially Breezy.

"Lindsay has every right to put her feet wherever she wants to put them," Tory Hibbs suddenly chimed in, glaring up at Breezy. "You don't own the school."

Tory Hibbs reminded Kim of some kind of bug. She made you want to squash her, Kim thought — especially since she had become a fringe member of the "cool" clique. Now she was unbearable. And she echoed everything Lindsay said. It was as though she never had a thought of her own. She was worse than a shadow — she was more like a clone. And one Lindsay Cunningham was bad enough. One and a half was a little out of hand.

"Oh, I don't own the school, but *you* do?" Breezy yelled, her crutch still poised in midair.

Kim knew that set in Breezy's shoulders. It meant that she was getting mighty mad. Kim also knew that Breezy's tolerance level, which was never very high, was especially low where Lindsay was concerned, and it was even lower than usual because of her injury. At that moment, it looked to Kim as if Breezy would like to club both Lindsay and Tory over the head with her crutches. Things were getting ugly.

"Lindsay, Tory, it's been fun," Kim cut in smoothly, giving Breezy a gentle but meaningful shove forward — it would not be cool to tip Breezy over. "But we've really got to run. Sorry we can't stay to chat more. We'll just have to pick this up later — like maybe some night in a back alley," she tossed over her shoulder.

"Good line, Kim," Breezy said, complimenting her as the two girls approached the Parrots table. "Two points."

"How dare that freckle face pip-squeak threaten you like that, Linz!" Kim heard Tory exclaim loudly.

"Freckle face pip-squeak?" Kim echoed as she slid into her seat next to Jazz. "That's a new one. Tory Hibbs is getting creative on us. She could be dangerous."

"I can't believe you're just going to sit back and take that, Kim," Breezy said, banging her hand angrily on the table. "Let's go back there and give it right back to them."

"It's not worth the energy, Breeze," Kim replied

good-naturedly, smiling at her friend. "Anyway, Tory Hibbs is no beauty queen. So she's really one to talk. On top of that, who's calling whom a pip-squeak? It's not like she rivals Manute Bol for tallest person in the NBA or anything, you know."

"Kim's right. They're just a bunch of knuckleheads!" Terry agreed, stuffing a big bite of mashed potatoes into her mouth. "If only life were like a horror movie, they'd go to sleep, dream about Freddy Kreuger, and never wake up."

"Who's Freddy again?" Jazz asked, taking a sip of her diet soda, her forehead wrinkled in confusion. "Is he the guy who walks around in a hockey mask in those *Halloween* movies? I didn't think he killed people when they were dreaming."

"No, Jazz," Breezy said, turning to her cousin in exasperation. "That's Michael Myers."

"Freddy's the scary dude from all the *Nightmare on Elm Street* movies," Kim explained.

"Oh, yeah," Jazz said and smiled. "Now, I remember. He's really, really ugly, too. Major scars on his face, right? Gro-o-ss."

"Of course he's ugly, he's in a horror movie," Breezy said, sounding more than a little impatient. "Geesh!"

"Why are you always picking on me?" Jazz asked, pouting.

"Hey, guys. You've got to see this new dance step

Richard and I learned last night," Kim cut in, feeling as if she was at home breaking up a fight between the twins or something. "Some guy at his school taught him. Are you ready?" Kim jumped up and pushed her chair in.

"Go, Kim. Go, Kim," Breezy and Terry started chanting, giving her a beat.

Kim loved to dance. She and her brother tried to teach themselves everything they saw on MTV. They even learned this one incredibly difficult step. She would move a little past Richard and hook her foot around his. Then they would spin around, their feet hooked together. It took a lot of balance. After they unhooked, Kim turned to Richard and leaped toward him. Then she bounced off his chest. It was definitely a hip-hop move.

Clearing her throat, Kim looked at her friends. "I need total silence for this move, please — except the beat," she joked. "Here we go!"

Starting with her basic step, where she did this thing that looked like a backward skip, Kim suddenly grabbed her right foot with her left hand. Then she jumped her right leg with her left foot. When she landed, she held up her arms, ready for the applause.

"Wow!" Jazz said when Kim stopped. "Is that hard?"

"I thought I was going to break my nose trying to learn it last night," Kim admitted, sitting back down in her chair. "I kept missing."

"I think you're better than M.C. Hammer," Jazz said.

"Can you teach me that later?" Crystal asked. Crystal, as an incredible ballet dancer, had the best rhythm on the Parrots. She and Kim liked to compare dance steps. Crystal didn't watch much MTV, but she still wanted to learn the dances.

Just then there was loud banging at the front of the cafeteria. "Quiet everybody!" a girl's voice shrilled. "I have an important announcement to make."

Kim craned her head to see toward the front of the room. Lindsay was standing on a chair by the cash registers and Tory, Molly Cooper, Gwen Billings, and Beth Douglas were clustered behind her. Kim thought their lineup looked kind of like Diana Ross and the Supremes, or something. They just needed some wigs and glitter gowns and they'd be good to go.

"Quiet!" Lindsay shrilled again.

There was an ear-piercing whistle, and Joey Carpenter stood up on his chair. "You heard her," he said loudly. "Shut up!"

"Joey is such a sucker," Breezy commented. "He's like Lindsay's puppy dog, or something."

"She does have him on a short leash, that's for sure," Kim pointed out. "But they do deserve each other, don't you think?"

"Really," echoed Terry.

"Quiet!" Lindsay shrilled again. "I have an important announcement to make."

"Uh-oh," Kim whispered. "This is going to be good."

"I am in charge of a committee to host what will definitely be the most incredible event of the school year," Lindsay began smugly.

"Hmmm," Terry said. "If she's in charge, I'm not going."

"You can count me out, too," Breezy added.

"Shhh, guys," Jazz cut in. "Listen."

"The seventh grade of Eleanor Roosevelt Junior High is going to be holding its first dance contest," Lindsay blurted out with a smile.

There were whistles and cheers all over the room.

"A dance contest?" Jazz squealed. "That's so exciting! I can't wait! Kim, you'll definitely win!"

"All couples must give me their names by next Wednesday," Lindsay went on smugly, tossing her white blonde hair over her shoulders. Kim was surprised her neck didn't go into spasm with all that flipping and tossing going on. "So, you better hurry up and get your partners," Lindsay concluded with a giggle.

"I think we should boycott," Terry said seriously, popping a piece of gum into her mouth.

"But the dinner is for a good cause," Kim pointed out. "Raising money for gym equipment and library books and stuff. Besides, I love to dance!"

"That's true," Crystal agreed, nodding.

"What do the winners get?" Desmond asked loudly,

standing up on his chair and staring at Lindsay.

"Good question, Des," Kim commented to the Parrots table. "That dude is really thinking."

"The winners get gift certificates to Music Maze," Lindsay announced with yet another flip of her hair.

"Hey, I might have to reconsider," Terry said. "Music Maze is a pretty cool record store."

"Oh, I really want to win, but there's no way I can with you in the contest, Kim," Jazz moaned. "I wonder which guy in our grade is the best dancer. I've got to ask him. Maybe that will help me."

"Hey, don't forget we have a big game against Mitchell Lumber the morning after this stupid contest," Breezy suddenly said. "I wonder if you all should even go to the dance."

"What do you mean, *you*?" Kim asked, looking over at Breezy. "Since when aren't you going?"

"Since I messed up my knee," Breezy said grumpily. "I don't think there are too many people known to have won dance contests on crutches, Kim."

"Hey, Breeze, I like that," Kim replied, disregarding the frown on Breezy's face. "You could bring a whole new dimension to the dance contest experience by introducing a totally new style of movement. Your four legs, so to speak, might even give you an advantage over everybody else's two," she finished with a grin.

Breezy's frown turned into a grin in return. "Yardley,

you are more than warped," Breezy said. "You are truly whacked."

"We *have* to go," Jazz said. "It's going to be really fun."

"We probably should," Crystal added after a slight pause. "School spirit and all that."

"I wonder who's going to end up going with whom," Jazz continued, her eyes lighting up at the prospect. "Just think. We're all going to have dates."

"Well, I have a date with Mr. Carrea right about now," Kim said, pushing back her chair. "So, I'll see you all later at practice."

"Going to social studies isn't a date, silly," Jazz said, looking at Kim as if she was crazy. "But I bet *You Know Who* is going to ask you, Kim. I bet he will."

"Who?" Breezy asked, staring at Kim.

"Nobody," Kim replied, as she felt herself blushing.

"Oooh, you're blushing," Jazz kidded Kim. "That's a dead giveaway. I knew you liked him. I just knew it."

"Jazz, I'm not blushing," Kim countered quickly. "That's just my natural rosy glow you're seeing."

"Yeah, right," Terry said, raising an eyebrow at Kim.

"So, who's the dude?" Breezy asked again.

"Jace Jeffries," Jazz breathed before Kim could even open her mouth.

"Jace from Ten Pin?" Breezy sputtered. "The catcher with all the attitude who didn't tag me out the other day when I got hurt?"

"That's him," Jazz said. "And he likes Kim."

"You like him?" Breezy asked Kim, a totally shocked expression on her face. "I never would have thought he was your type."

"I never said I liked him," Kim retorted, blushing again.

"You're blushing again," Jazz commented. "See, I told you so."

"Jace? Kim?" Breezy asked, looking at Kim and shaking her head. "I never would have figured."

"Oooohhh, you have to get him to ask you to be his partner for the dance contest," Jazz said. "That would be the perfect way for you two to hook up."

"Sounds serious, Kim," Terry put in with a smile. "Jazz is going to be all over you about this one. She has that look in her eye."

"Either way, the most important thing is that you guys win the game against Mel's Auto Body," Breezy commented, suddenly serious. "We can't let them beat us. We have to win."

Kim looked up to find Breezy's dark eyes focused on her. She knew, without Breezy having to say a single word, that the look meant it was up to relief captain Kim to guarantee the win. And she would. Kim had never let Breezy down before and she wasn't about to start now. Especially since baseball and the Parrots were really important to her, too.

5

"Let's go over the plan one more time," Breezy said, wiping a smudge of chocolate off her chin with a napkin. "You've all got to concentrate really, really hard on this game. Mel's has an incredible lineup. You know, Peter Tolhurst loves fastballs."

"Yeah, he eats them for breakfast instead of cereal," Kim agreed, taking a sip of her strawberry milk shake. "But we all know that I throw that incredible 100 mile-per-hour fastball guaranteed to burn a hole in any bat," she joked. "He might not love my fastball."

It was after practice on Friday afternoon and the Parrots were at the Neptune, the diner Jazz's parents owned, discussing their strategy for their big game against Mel's Auto Body the following day.

"Kim, stop fooling around," Breezy admonished with a frown, tightening her dark-blonde ponytail and glaring at her friend.

"Fooling around? Are you saying that you think I can't throw a fastball that travels 100 miles per hour?"

Kim asked in mock disbelief, blowing her red bangs off her forehead. "Nice faith. Real nice."

They'd had a really rough practice. At least Breezy hadn't been there, Kim thought, or she would have had a cow. They hadn't been able to get anything going, and no matter what Kim did to boost spirits, it seemed as if nobody had wanted to concentrate. Breezy, meanwhile, had been at physical therapy and Kim could tell that she was not in a good mood. Kim could understand how frustrated she must feel at not being able to play in an important game. But she didn't know what she could tell her to make her feel better. Clearly, kidding around was not the way to go.

Breezy had made the Parrots work hard all week. It was as if now that she couldn't play, she was throwing all of her energy into making the Parrots work harder than ever — especially Kim. Plus, she had had Kim practice all these complicated pitches over and over again almost every day this week. Kim's entire right side was sore — from shoulder to wrist.

Breezy kept drilling her over and over as if she could turn Kim into Dwight Gooden overnight, or something. It wasn't going to work. Kim was lucky to get the ball over the plate, much less worry about the position of her fingers or the speed of the pitch. But she'd kept her temper, as usual. Now, though, she was beginning to feel a little worn out, especially after trying to make Jazz pay attention, Betsy run a little faster for the ball, and Andrea connect better with unexpected pitches. She couldn't help it, though, if she wasn't Breezy and couldn't get the same results trying to get the Parrots to give it all they had in practice.

"Kim, this is serious," Breezy practically snapped, her dark eyes blazing. "I mean, we cannot afford to lose this game. You know that."

"I know, Breezy," Kim replied with a sigh. Sometimes her friend had no sense of humor. I guess baseball was just one of those things she couldn't joke about. "You keep saying that."

Kim sighed again. She couldn't help it. She had no energy. The week had been really hectic because her mother was away and her father had worked late almost every night. And she'd had her hands full with tons of homework and keeping an eye on the kids. Kim felt tired just thinking about it all.

"We get the picture, Breezy," Terry cut in, leaning back against the booth. "You know we plan to give 'em all we've got tomrrow. We always do, don't we?"

"And I'll go over all the stats again tonight," Crystal put in earnestly, giving Breezy a small smile.

"Oh, that reminds me," Breezy said, turning to Kim. "You've got to watch out for that tall skinny kid with the black crew cut. You know, the one who always gets like A-plus plus on every quiz in our math class."

"A-plus plus?" Jazz asked in confusion. "I didn't know there was such a grade."

Breezy groaned and turned toward her cousin.

"There's not really," Terry cut Breezy off before she could say anything. "She was just exaggerating."

"Oh, you mean, Lou Aversano?" Kim asked, twisting her straw wrapper around her ring finger. "He's always spoiling the curve. Why can't he get something wrong once in a while?"

"He's very good defensively," Breezy replied.

"I didn't know there was such a thing as defensive math," Kim said, grinning. Sometimes an opportunity came up that she just couldn't resist — whether Breezy liked baseball jokes or not. "I've heard of defensive driving, good football defense, but defensive math? Never heard of it."

Crystal, Jazz, and Terry all cracked up, but Breezy quieted them down quickly with a short, "Kim!" When everyone had stopped laughing, Breezy continued. "This is serious. Lou plays third base and he covers the hot corner like Wade Boggs."

"We've played Mel's before," Terry said, beginning to sound impatient. "Lou is a great third baseman. We know that. Don't worry about it, Breeze. We've got it covered."

"Yeah, but Kim didn't have to pitch to him before," Breezy replied. "He's a pitcher's nightmare — the total singles hitter. He can hit anything. So when you pitch to him, you probably want to stick with your change-up, Kim."

Kim just looked at her friend and nodded helplessly. What change-up, she couldn't help thinking. How in the world could she worry about the finer points of pitching, like the speed of the ball and catching the batter off guard with an off-speed ball, when it was anyone's guess if the pitch would even come anywhere near the plate? Sure, she had a good throwing arm and could easily peg a runner at first, but throwing from the mound was an entirely different game, no matter what Breezy might like to think. She couldn't explain that to Breezy, though. Breezy just expected Kim to be able to do it — she didn't care how.

"And you have to watch out for their pitcher, Desmond McGraw," Breezy said, continuing on as if the whole pitching matter was settled, eyeing each of the Parrots. "He throws the sneakiest change-up. If you can predict it, it's no problem. But the dude's got an incredible delivery — he acts as if he's going to throw a rocket every time. And then, boom, it's a granny change-up."

"Oooh, I know who he is," Jazz put in suddenly, eating a spoonful of whipped cream off her banana split. "He's really cute. Beth Douglas has a major crush on him and the other day I heard her in the bathroom telling Lindsay and Gwen that she wanted to ask him to be her partner for the dance contest because he's supposedly a totally great dancer —"

"Jazz, I don't really care about this dance, okay?" Breezy interrupted, sounding more than a little snippy as she drummed her fingers against the table and frowned at her cousin.

"But you're the one who brought up the subject in the first place," Jazz pointed out, not backing down.

"Hey, guys," Kim cut in, looking from Breezy to Jazz. They were more alike than Breezy thought. They were both very stubborn. "Will you two please stop fighting? It's played already. Totally."

"But, she —" Breezy and Jazz began at the same time.

The two of them sounded like Josh and Jenny the way they bickered. At least Josh and Jenny had an excuse. They were only 6 years old, after all.

"Oh my gosh!" Kim exclaimed suddenly. Talking about the twins reminded her of her family and her responsibilities at home. "I just remembered. I'm supposed to go to Faith's dress rehearsal tonight. What time is it now?"

"Five-oh-six," Jazz replied slowly, looking down at her Mickey Mouse digital watch.

"Oh, no. I was supposed to pick up the twins at five. I've got to run, guys," Kim blurted out, grabbing her practice bag off the floor and wriggling out of the booth.

"Hey, wait a minute," Breezy said in protest. "This game is very important. You can't just blow it off like that. When are you going to practice those pitches we talked about? I thought you were coming over to my house after dinner."

"I have to get the kids," Kim continued quickly

without meeting Breezy's eyes. "I'll talk to you later."

With that Kim flew out of the diner, the bell jangling loudly behind her. She didn't even have her bike because she'd gotten a flat the day before and hadn't had time to fix it. She'd just have to run, and hope Josh and Jenny weren't too upset. But they always sulked when they were picked up late and acted as if they had been forgotten. Which they never were, of course.

Kim had to admit to herself, though, that she *had* kind of forgotten about them for a little while. But that was only because she had so many other things on her mind. At least she had finished sewing Faith's costume for the play. Her mother had designed it. It was a lacy white cotton dress with a pink sash — perfect for Faith's role as Becky Thatcher in the fifth-grade production of *Tom Sawyer*. Kim had even thrown it into the washing machine that morning with a little bleach to make sure it was totally white. Now all she had to do was pop it in the dryer and then iron it.

"Hey, Red," a voice suddenly cut into Kim's thoughts. "Where are you going in such a big hurry?"

Kim turned quickly as Jace Jeffries pulled up next to her on a brand-new red and white all-terrain bike. He was wearing faded blue jeans and a white T-shirt, and his long dark hair was slicked back off his face. He looked great — kind of like Marlon Brando in that old black and white movie her dad had rented about some motorcycle gang. Kim forgot what it was called — the Wild Something — but her dad said it was his favorite movie. Marlon Brando was really young in the movie and he was so cool looking.

"So, Red, you want a ride?" Jace asked, running his hand through his hair and grinning at her.

"Uh . . . I'm in a big rush," Kim said and gulped as she found herself staring into those incredible grey-blue eyes once again. "Besides, where would I sit?"

"Well, I'll just stand and pedal and you can sit," Jace said, patting the seat. "Besides, wherever you're going, you'll definitely get there faster on this."

Kim had to agree that he was right about that even if she still thought he was a macho jerk. The most important thing was to get going already. "Okay, thanks," Kim said. A ride was a ride, after all — no matter who was doing the driving.

"You can hold onto me for balance," Jace continued in a businesslike tone after she had climbed up behind him.

"I happen to have incredible balance," Kim retorted, a little shortly. Riding a bike was not exactly a new thing for her. "Besides, I can hold onto the back of the seat if I need to."

Shrugging, Jace pushed off and began pedaling. Kim, with nothing to hold on to, quickly slipped to the right. Knowing they were going to fall unless she regained her balance, she grabbed onto the seat and righted herself.

"Now, where are you going?" he asked.

"Hudson Terrace," Kim replied. "Off Main."

"No problem," Jace said as he turned down Main and headed down a steep hill, not bothering to brake at all. Kim smiled and then laughed out loud as they went faster and faster. She loved speed. She also had to admit that Jace was right about holding on. It definitely made for a safer ride.

In a matter of what felt like seconds to Kim but was actually more like minutes, they were there. Kim hopped off the bike and grinned at Jace. "Um . . . thanks for the ride," she mumbled, feeling her face get red. "I really appreciate it."

"It was no biggie," Jace replied. "I take every opportunity to ride on this thing. I just got it."

"I love it," Kim agreed with a smile, still feeling flushed. "It really goes fast down hills. What a rush!"

"Yeah," said Jace. "So, Kim," he began and then hesitated, looking down at his handlebars. "I wanted to know if you . . . uh . . . wanted to go —"

"You're late," two voices suddenly interrupted their conversation. "Late, late, late!"

Kim spun around. Josh and Jenny were standing on the sidewalk, their identical green and orange Ninja Turtle lunch boxes in their hands and their matching Turtle backpacks on their shoulders. "Hi, guys," Kim joked. "How're you doing?"

Josh and Jenny both stuck their tongues out at her and didn't say anything.

"Your brother and sister?" Jace asked.

Kim nodded and walked over to where the two kids were standing. "They look a lot like you," Jace continued, suddenly sounding really nice.

"Okay, guys, I have a riddle. Are you ready?" Kim questioned, bending down to ruffle their hair.

Josh and Jenny just looked at her expectantly. Thank goodness for jokes, Kim thought to herself. Nobody could stay mad for long if they were laughing.

"What did one wall say to the other wall?" she asked. She knew for a fact that it was the twins' favorite riddle.

"Meetcha at the corner," Josh and Jenny chorused in unison, as they cracked up.

"That's right," she said. "And now we better rock and roll around this corner if we want to eat dinner and make it to Faith's play on time."

"Hey, Kim, we'll pick this up where we left off tomorrow," Jace said, turning his bike around. "Like the joke."

"Thanks again," Kim replied with another smile. People were so funny, she thought. Everyone said Jace had so much attitude and he did, but if you didn't buy into it, he was an okay guy. That was Kim's policy — be nice to someone and they'll be nice back to you. It worked almost all the time.

"Okay, guys, let's make like bananas and split," Kim joked, grabbing hold of each kid's hand.

As they rounded the corner to Willow Street where

the Yardleys lived, Kim thought about Jace. She didn't like him in the way Jazz said she did, but she liked the thought that she'd been able to get to the nicer person lurking beneath all the attitude. Under normal circumstances, she would have thought about telling Breezy about him and how it had seemed as if he was about to ask her to be his partner for the dance contest, but Breezy would probably think it was stupid because it had nothing to do with baseball. And since Breezy couldn't play right now, baseball was all she thought about. Anyway, Breezy didn't even want any of them to go to the dance contest in the first place.

As soon as Kim opened the door, her good mood faded fast. There were dirty glasses and plates piled up all around the kitchen sink, along with a half-gallon container of chocolate ice cream that had dripped all over the counter. Red was sitting on one of the kitchen chairs, eating potato chips out of an open bag on the table. And the song *Ice Ice Baby*, by Vanilla Ice, was blaring loudly from the family room. There was no one in sight, but Kim had a very good idea about who was responsible for the mess.

"Richard Yardley!" Kim yelled. "Get out here this instant!" She walked over to the refrigerator and got one of her mother's chicken cassseroles out of the freezer. Then she turned on the oven and popped it inside.

Josh and Jenny stared at her without moving, their blue eyes wide. They weren't used to an angry Kim, she knew. She almost never lost her temper. Why bother? Life was too short. But this was a major mess, and Richard wasn't going to get away with it.

"My life is over!" a high voice squealed suddenly.

"Faith, don't be ridiculous," Kim said, turning around to face her sister who had just walked up the basement steps. "The only person in this house whose life is over is Richard . . ." she continued, but then let her voice trail off. Faith was holding her Becky Thatcher dress at arm's length as if it were some kind of slimy swamp creature that she didn't want to touch.

"What happened to your dress?" Kim asked directly.

"I don't know," Faith replied, blinking back the tears. "You're the one who washed it. And now look at it. Just look at it," she sobbed. "It's totally ruined."

"It's no big deal," Kim said, trying to sound a lot more confident that she felt. "So, it's . . . um . . . got some blue and red, uh, accents now," she continued weakly, racking her brains to think of something to make Faith feel better. "Faith, just think, you'll be giving Becky Thatcher a whole new look — tie-dye. You'll be a Becky for the Nineties."

That only made Faith cry harder. Finally, she brushed back a damp auburn curl and hiccupped twice. She fixed her watery blue eyes on Kim as if her heart was breaking. "They didn't have tie-dye when Tom Sawyer lived. Now I can't be in the play at all. And it's all your fault," Faith continued, bursting into tears once again. Then she ran out of the room and slammed the door.

"What's with her?" Richard asked, sauntering around the corner into the kitchen. "Break a fingernail, or something?"

"Richard, would you like to explain what you think you're doing?" Kim hissed, glaring at her brother.

"I wish I could," Richard replied, pulling a can of soda out of the refrigerator. "Me and Rob and B.J. have been trying to figure out our math homework all afternoon. It's been total torture," he added, popping the top off the soda, and throwing it toward the garbage can. It landed with a clink on the linoleum floor instead. "If I could explain it, there'd be no problem."

Kim just stared at him, clenching and unclenching her fists by her sides. She exhaled quickly three times trying to stay calm.

"Hey, don't look so bent out of shape," Richard added with a cocky grin. "Even Michael Jordan misses a shot once in a while. I'm sure the NBA will still draft me."

"Richard, don't do this to me," Kim yelled, inhaling sharply. She fought very hard against the incredible urge she was having to grab the can of soda out of his hand and dump it over his head.

"What's with you?" Richard retorted, staring at Kim as if she had two heads, or something. "Women. They're all crazy. Huh, Josh?" he added, turning to his little brother and holding up his hand to give him a high five.

"Yeah, dude," Josh agreed with a giggle, high-fiving

Richard back as Vanilla Ice sang, "Ice ice baby."

"Richard, if you don't turn off that music and clean this place up within seconds I'm going to . . . to . . . to put *you* on ice," Kim sputtered. She pressed her temples with her fingers. She had to stay calm. She had to cope. She would. She always did.

"No problemo," Richard replied, saluting Kim with his right hand and clicking his heels together. "Your wish is my command."

"Something smells funny," Jenny said suddenly, wrinkling her nose and squinting her eyes.

"Yeah, something smells bad," Josh agreed, nodding.

"The chicken casserole," Kim moaned. "Oh no, it's burning." She sprang toward the oven and turned it off. "Hey, who set this dial to 550?" Kim questioned, frowning at Richard.

"Hey, don't look at me," Richard said.

Just then the smoke alarm went off, its piercing sound echoing loudly through the house. Red started to howl; Ninja, the cat, went back out the cat door she'd just come through, and Josh and Jenny put their hands over their ears and scampered out of the room. Kim shook her head and opened the kitchen door and windows to let some of the smoke escape. She couldn't believe the chaos that suddenly seemed to have taken over her life. How had everything gotten so out of control?

6

Kim woke up to the sound of music. Faith's alarm clock had gone off loudly. Of course, Faith hadn't moved to turn it off. She probably liked the Madonna song that was blaring. Madonna was Kim's least favorite singer — Kim didn't think she could carry a tune if she had a bucket.

Burying her head underneath her pillow, Kim squeezed her eyes shut and tried to block out the music. She'd just been having the worst nightmare. Breezy had turned into this pterodactyl bird and Mr. Krasnow was a vampire bat and Faith was a vulture and Jazz was a seagull and they were all chasing her around the baseball field squawking like crazy, and trying to peck her to death because she hadn't done something she was supposed to. The thing was she had no idea what it was she was supposed to have been doing in the first place.

Kim groaned suddenly, remembering something Crystal had mentioned to her after she read a book on dreams. Crystal had told her that everyone in her dreams was really her, that they all represented different parts of her. Kim hated to think she was part crow or vulture. Really weird. Too weird for this early in the morning.

Kim bolted up in bed. "Oh my gosh!" she exclaimed to the motionless lump underneath the pink and yellow quilt on the other side of the room. "Faith, wake up! That music is so loud I feel like I'm in a bad video, or something. Meanwhile, what time is it? My clock stopped at three-thirty-seven."

Kim hopped out of bed, pulling her black and orange Baltimore Orioles nightshirt down, as she grabbed the old white sweat socks she wore as slippers off the dark brown hardwood floor. Then she took a running leap for her sister's bed. She landed with a soft thud somewhere by Faith's ankles. Faith jumped up as if she had been shot, just as Kim hit the button on the clock to turn the music off.

"What's going on, Kim?" Faith asked sleepily, rubbing her eyes. "Is it my cue to go on stage?"

"No, silly," Kim replied, smiling at her sister. "It's time to get up. And I'm running totally late because I overslept."

"Hey, what did you really think of last night?" Faith prodded, sinking back against her pillows. "Was I the best Becky Thatcher you've ever seen?"

"Definitely," Kim said immediately, bounding off her sister's bed. "Although it might have been the dress that did it."

Kim and Faith looked at each other and giggled. In her frantic state the night before, Kim had done the only thing she could think of to do under the circumstances. She had thrown the dress back into the washing machine, but this time with everything red in the house — red sweats, red socks, red towels. The dress had turned totally pink after that so that you could hardly notice the blue splotches from her first laundry fiasco.

"Hey, I've really got to hurry," Kim continued, going over to the closet the two girls shared. "Have you seen my uniform anywhere, Faith?"

"Hmmm," Faith murmured, looking into space as she lay against her pillows. She reached for the radio and turned it back on. A new Madonna song was just beginning.

"Earth to Faith, Earth to Faith," Kim continued, turning to stare at her sister. She shook her head, trying not to listen to the next Madonna song. It must be some kind of music marathon. Either way it was worse than Chinese water torture. She had enough to worry about. "Pay attention to me for a minute. I have a big game today against Mel's Auto Body so I'm going to be gone until about four. I was thinking you could take the dynamic duo to the park first thing this morning —"

"What?!" Faith exploded, throwing her covers back. "I have rehearsal in an hour. I can't baby-sit."

"Oh, all right," Kim sighed, turning back to the closet. "I guess Richard can do it then." She could barely keep up with her own schedule. She had no idea how her mother kept up with what everyone was doing all the time.

Kim pawed through all the stuff that was hanging on what was supposed to be her side of the closet, but she couldn't find her uniform anywhere. Faith's clothes were strewn all over her side, too. Faith was so sloppy. She even had clothes lying all over the bottom of the closet, on top of their shoes. Kim could not imagine being so disorganized. It was a wonder Faith could ever find anything. Almost never bothered by the mess, Kim got upset only when she couldn't find something. Like now.

Kim turned away from the closet in disgust. She tried to think of where her uniform could be. She knew she hadn't worn it since their game last Saturday against Ten Pin Bowling. Boy, it would be great to win again, Kim thought with a smile as she remembered her double. She'd done pretty well taking over at that game when Breezy had been hurt.

But she hadn't had to pitch in that game. Kim had to admit she was worried about having to pitch. But she would give it her all. And she'd show Breezy just how well she could pitch when she really tried. There was no way she was going to let Breezy and the Parrots down. Concentration was the key, Kim decided. That, plus a little luck, and she'd be fine.

Kim looked through her drawers in the big yellow wooden dresser she and Faith shared. Her uniform was nowhere to be found — not even in the huge pile of pink clothing lying all over the top of the dresser.

Pink happened to be Faith's favorite color, a fact which sometimes got on Kim's nerves because she hated pink almost as much as Breezy did. So much of Faith's stuff was pink, like her pillows, her trash can, her teddy bears, her notebooks. Kim liked navy-blue and red.

As a last resort, Kim went back to the closet and began to go through the stuff that Faith had left lying all over the floor.

"Faith!" Kim exclaimed suddenly, holding her uniform up and shaking it in her sister's direction. "How did this get in with your junk?"

"I don't know," Faith said and shrugged.

"Well, that's just great," Kim replied, shaking her head. "My first day as captain and I have to wear a dirty uniform."

"It's not my fault," Faith snapped. "You're the one who's supposed to be so neat."

Kim groaned. She was not about to get into a fight with Faith over something stupid like a dirty uniform. So it had some grass stains and some mud on it? Big deal. Kim needed to feel tough anyway for her pitching debut. Really great players always ended up getting dirt on their uniforms. So she'd start out with some dirt, too. It couldn't hurt. She thought she would need every bit of help she could get, and a rough and tough attitude wouldn't be bad at all.

Kim dashed down the stairs. She knew she really had to get moving. She was supposed to be at the field early to discuss strategy with Breezy and Ro, and go over the stats. Breezy almost always got to games before any of the other Parrots did, and Kim knew that as the substitute captain, she had better be there early, too. The pressure of it all, Kim thought, giggling. But, hey, she was tough and her mind was like steel. A little pressure couldn't bend her will to win.

"Hey, Richie-Poo," Kim said, bounding into the kitchen where Richard and the twins were sitting around the table eating cereal.

"Uh-oh," Richard replied, looking up suspiciously. "I know that tone. It means that you want something. So the answer is no, of course."

"Give me a break," Kim said, grabbing the orange juice container out of the refrigerator and kicking the door shut with one of her sneakers.

"No again," Richard retorted, his mouth full of cereal. "I can read you like a book and the answer is no: n-o."

"Well, that's too bad," Kim retorted, her face flushing in anger. "Because you don't have a choice. I have a big game against Mel's Auto Body in less than an hour, so you're just going to have to take care of the twins. I can't do it."

Josh and Jenny licked their upper lips where they both had milk mustaches. Then they looked from Kim to Richard and back to Kim.

"So, Kimbo, you're taking care of the twins today, right?" Mr. Yardley boomed as he walked into the kitchen, brushing a shaggy lock of red hair, the same shade as his children's, out of his eyes. "Rich is helping me at the garage for a while and I definitely can't have the kids there. They might get hurt. Then he has a soccer game. And Faith has rehearsal, doesn't she?"

"Uh-huh," Kim muttered, glaring at her brother.

"You're just the person for the job," Richard assured his sister with a wink. "The twins will cheer for you. Right, dudes?"

"Right, dude," Josh and Jenny said and giggled.

"Is that all right, Kim?" her father asked seriously. "I mean, we still might be able to hire a sitter if it's going to be a problem. Or Mrs. McManus next door might be able to put up with these terrors for a few hours."

"No problem, Dad," Kim answered quickly, glaring at her brother again. She knew there wasn't a lot of extra money around to pay for a sitter when she could take care of the twins. And Josh and Jenny hated Mrs. McManus — they thought she smelled like mothballs and she yelled all the time. Besides, her father had enough stuff to worry about. She wasn't about to bug him now, especially with Mom away.

But how did it always happen, she wondered, that she got stuck with all of the responsibility all of the time? It wasn't fair, but then again lots of things in the world weren't fair. Or so grown-ups were always saying. She'd just have to keep the kids in the dugout and hope that they behaved. It was the only way. She could handle it. No problemo.

After breakfast Mr. Yardley gave Kim and the twins a ride to the field. Kim wasn't an hour early, as she had promised Breezy she would be, but at least the game wasn't starting for almost 15 minutes. That should be plenty of time to go over whatever last-minute pearls of wisdom Breezy felt like dishing out. Besides, there wasn't much Breezy knew about baseball that Kim didn't. That was probably why they were such good friends.

"Where have you been?" Breezy yelled as soon as she spotted Kim. "And what are *they* doing here?" she continued, glaring down at Josh and Jenny as if they were alien beings.

"Don't have a cow, Breeze," Kim replied calmly. "I overslept, which is why I'm late. And I brought the dynamic duo because I thought it was about time we started a cheerleading squad. See, both kids are wearing pink T-shirts."

"This is not funny, Kim," Breezy retorted, leaning heavily on one crutch and pointing the other one at Kim. "Mel's is a tough team and we already have one handicap. We don't exactly have room for two more."

"Lighten up, Breezy," Kim continued, unphased. "They'll just be hanging out in the dugout."

"What?" Breezy exploded, her face turning red in

anger. "We can't have two little kids sitting in the dugout. It's totally unprofessional. We might get disqualified. Plus, they'll disrupt everyone's concentration. No way, Kim."

"Well, that's too bad," Kim retorted, thinking that this wasn't as easy as she had thought it was going to be. "If they go, I go."

Breezy was silent for a moment. She stared at Kim, her dark eyes blazing. Kim stared back. One thing she had learned early on in her friendship with Breezy was that she couldn't back down. Breezy had a tendency to run roughshod over people — completely unconsciously. She just thought there was only one way of doing things — her way. So Kim made a point of showing her that there were very often at least two sides to a situation, if not more. As far as she was concerned, this was one of those times.

"Hey, Kim," a voice suddenly interrupted them. "I wanted to wish you luck," said Oscar as he walked over to where the two girls were standing.

"Thanks, Oscar," Kim replied. "I don't need luck, though. The ghost of Dizzy Dean will see me through this game."

"Forget it, Kim," Breezy yelled, obviously fed up with Kim's joking for the moment. "Just forget it. Do whatever you want. Get us disqualified. Thanks a lot." With that she stormed away, her crutches moving furiously across the field.

"Whoa! Was it something I said?" Oscar asked Kim, with concern.

"It's us," Josh said solemnly. "Breezy said we were hubcaps."

"Handicaps," Kim corrected her brother with a giggle. "Breezy's all bent out of shape because I have to watch Josh and Jenny and I wanted them to sit in the dugout. She claims we'll get disqualified, or something. But I think she's just ticked because she can't play and we're playing against Peter's team. Oh, and she's probably worried that I'll throw like a no-hitter or something, and I'll become the new star pitcher in the league and she'll be relegated to the position of manager or batboy, I mean batgirl."

"Well, they can sit with me in the bleachers," Oscar suggested, with a smile. "I mean, if they want to, that is."

"Thanks, Oscar," Kim replied immediately. "You're a totally groovy dude." She giggled at her own expression. She and Breezy had once heard this girl saying it about some new boyfriend she had. They had thought it was the funniest thing.

Oscar blushed and pushed his glasses farther up on his nose. "It's no big deal," he added, kicking his black high top into the dirt. "But, groovy dude? Kim, don't date yourself."

"I'm feel-ing groov-y today, O," Kim retorted. She could say goofy stuff like that to Oscar because *he* had a sense of humor — even on game days. "Well, I better rock," she said, smiling at Oscar again.

"Good luck!" Oscar repeated and then turned to the twins. "So what do you think, guys? Popcorn, peanuts, hot dogs, soda? All of the above?"

"Yeah!" Josh and Jenny chorused together as they followed Oscar to the bleachers.

Kim shook her head and grinned as she sprinted across the field toward the Parrots dugout. Oscar was a great guy, she thought. He was really the best, even if the twins would have major stomach-aches later. Now she could totally focus on the game.

Taking a deep breath, Kim squared her shoulders and headed for the dugout, where Ro and Breezy were waiting for her. She knew that it could be ugly.

The game definitely began on an ugly note. Andrea Campbell, who played third and could at least hit consistently most of the time, was sick. Jazz was late, and when she finally showed, realized she had forgotten her glove.

Kim hoped things would get better once the first inning was underway, but it was not to be. Sarah Fishman, the relief pitcher who was starting because Breezy was out, couldn't get anything going and walked four of Mel's batters before the Parrots were finally able to retire the side.

The second and third innings were great examples of

what not to do in baseball. Kim couldn't believe the amount of errors that the Parrots committed, to say nothing of their performance at the plate. Three-up, three-down was taking on new meaning for Kim. They hadn't even made it through their lineup. It was unreal. How could one player make so much of a difference, Kim wondered.

By the bottom of the third, Mel's was leading by a score of 6-1. The lone Parrot run was Terry's. She'd slugged one over the fence, but because no other Parrots were on base, it remained their one and only run. On top of that, it had begun to drizzle.

"Kim!" Breezy said as she crutched over to her just before the beginning of the fourth inning. "We still have a chance. The game's only half over. You can turn this game around. I know you can."

Looking at Breezy, Kim thought her friend had a wild look in her eyes. Breezy was probably incredibly frustrated that she couldn't help her team out of the very deep hole they had dug themselves into.

"Show them what you've got, hon!" Ro encouraged, patting her on the back and smiling broadly as Kim grabbed her glove.

What she had, Kim thought with a grimace, was pretty scary. She was just hoping that her pitches would go in the general vicinity of home plate and it wouldn't be too, too embarrassing. Because the potential for it was definitely there.

Yawning yet again, Kim couldn't believe how tired she felt. And she couldn't seem to stop yawning. It was like a nervous reflex. She'd read somewhere that people yawn when they're stressed out because they need to get more oxygen to their brains, or something like that. Kim felt as if she needed an oxygen tent at this point. She shook her head to clear it. It would probably take more than oxygen to turn this game around. That was for sure.

"You can do it. Just think positively, Kim," Ro encouraged, putting her arm around her shoulders. "Think of the great pitchers of all time and summon their auras — Nolan Ryan, Orel Herscheiser, Roger Clemens, Jim Palmer, Dizzy Dean."

Kim looked at Ro and had to smile. Ro was decked out in her usual coach garb — zebra striped leggings and a neon-orange sweatshirt underneath her Pink Parrots jersey. How were the auras of great pitchers past and present really going to help her now?

Kim jogged out to the mound and kicked at the dirt with her cleats for a few moments. Finally, she stopped and faced Terry, who was crouching behind home plate. She was really between the devil and the deep blue sea here. If she warmed up, Mel's Auto Body would see just how bad she was. If she didn't, she'd pitch even worse because she wouldn't be warmed up and might even pull a muscle. Opting for warming up, Kim had a sudden thought that maybe it would work to her advantage. If Ten Pin saw her pitching, they might think that no one could be as bad as she was and assume she was just trying to psych them out by making them think she was really bad. Which she was.

Then Kim shrugged. What did it matter anyway, she wondered. She'd pitch how she pitched and that was that. Luckily, her warm-up pitches weren't too bad. Terry had this incredible knack of moving her glove, without seeming to move it, so the ball always looked as if it was landing where it was aimed. Which it wasn't.

Finally, the moment of truth arrived. Lou Aversano stepped into the batter's box, his tall body crouched as he got ready to bat. Terry waved at Kim and then tapped the inside of her leg with one finger. Kim wanted to look behind her because she felt as if Terry must be signaling to someone else. But she knew it wasn't true. Terry wanted her to throw a fastball.

Kim swung her arm a few times and tried to psych herself up. She thought of Dizzy Dean. She couldn't believe she was actually listening to Ro's advice about summoning up the auras of famous pitchers. Dizzy Dean was one of Kim's old favorites. He was a real character, with a crazy sense of humor — even about baseball. But he had something else — a smoking fastball. In 1934 he became the first major league pitcher to win 30 games in a season. Not a bad aura to receive, Kim figured. She squeezed her eyes shut for a second and summoned up his image. Not that she really knew what he looked like, but she could imagine.

All right, she thought to herself, she could do this, she really could. She and Dizzy were good to go. She opened her eyes and faced the plate.

Taking a deep breath, Kim went into her windup. She twisted her whole body and let the ball go. But it didn't zip speedily across the plate the way she had imagined. Instead, it moved kind of slowly to the outside corner and Lou, who had incredibly long arms and a long swing, connected with it solidly. The ball went flying toward rightfield as Lou took off for first base.

Kim slowly pivoted her head toward rightfield. She couldn't believe it — humiliated on her very first pitch! Jazz was not paying the closest attention to what was going on and the ball zoomed right over her head. She took off to get it and so did Julie from centerfield.

Wishing she could shut her eyes, Kim found herself unable to do so. She watched Lou continue to race around the bases, his long legs moving fast. Julie and Jazz, both in hot pursuit of the ball, bumped into each other as they simultaneously bent down to grab it and fell onto the field. Finally, Crystal rushed from first to get the ball. But it was too late. Lou had already made it home to major cheering from his team.

Catching Crystal's throw, Kim stared at the ball for a minute. This was definitely not going well. It wasn't only her pitching either — it was as if everyone's fielding got a little looser and sloppier without Breezy on the field yelling at all of them.

"Come on, Kimmie!" Ro shouted from the dugout. "Forget about it! Don't let it get to you! Just concentrate!"

Kim gulped and raised her eyes to look at Terry behind the plate. She could not let this get to her or she wouldn't have a prayer. But the score was now 7-1 and things were getting really ugly.

"Do it like we practiced, Kim!" Breezy yelled from the dugout. "Come on. Don't give up!"

Kim jammed her hat over her red braids and wiggled her fingers in her glove. Breezy was right, of course. But it was a lot easier to talk about it than to do it.

Peter Tolhurst stepped up to the plate. He grinned. She gulped. Peter was the best slugger in the entire league. She could only be thankful there were no other Mel's players on the bases. A home run is one thing — like Lou's. A grand slam home run was quite another.

Terry signaled for a change-up. Going into her windup, Kim offered a silent plea to Dizzy Dean and then delivered the pitch. It was very definitely a change-up in the sense that it changed speeds, but it was so far outside it needed a trail of breadcrumbs to find its way back to the plate.

"Ball one!" the umpire announced.

Kim sighed heavily and wished she had never agreed to pitch in the first place. It was just too much. She couldn't learn to pitch overnight. If only there was a tape she could play at night, like "Learn Proper Pitching Techniques While You Sleep," or something like that.

Terry signaled for a sidearm fastball. Racking her brain trying to remember how to throw that pitch, Kim took a minute to figure it out. Finally, she delivered. Kim was so busy admiring her pitch that she didn't realize quite how high it was until Terry stood all the way up in order to snag it.

"Ball two!" the umpire called.

"Come on, Kim," she heard Breezy yell. "Concentrate!"

Kim didn't even look up. She couldn't face Breezy. She knew she was really fouling things up, but she couldn't seem to help herself. She looked at Terry instead, who patted the inside of her leg with one finger. Kim couldn't believe it — Terry was signaling for an inside fastball. Kim was having trouble just getting the ball over the middle of the plate, she couldn't worry about the finer points of control that would let her nick corners. Shrugging, Kim decided to throw fastballs from then on in and just aim for the middle of the plate. At least then she'd have a chance of a getting a strike here or there.

It didn't happen on the next two pitches and Peter jogged to first on a base on balls, as Desmond McGraw approached the plate. Oh great, Kim thought, the change-up whiz. Maybe he couldn't hit. But as Kim discovered within seconds, he could hit just fine. With a touch almost as soft as Breezy's, Desmond bunted her first pitch a few feet up the third base line. Kim was standing back on her heels, not ready to run anywhere.

"Rats!" she exclaimed, rocking forward on her feet and running in to get Desmond's bunt. She was too slow and he'd already made it to first by the time she rifled the ball to Crystal. Why couldn't she pitch like that, she wondered. When she threw a pick-off throw, her aim was right on. It was just when she was on the mound facing a batter that she had problems.

"Kim, pay attention!" Breezy yelled from the dugout. That was easy for Breezy to say, Kim thought. She knew how to pitch. Kim was not having fun. And the thought that she was letting down her teammates was making everything that much worse. Dizzy Dean's aura was not helping out. Maybe she needed someone more modern.

Keith McAllister was up next. A short, wiry blond kid, Keith had beaten just about everyone in the running events at field day last year. Kim knew he was really, really fast.

Terry signaled for a sinker. A sinker, Kim thought, right. Opting for another fastball, Kim went into her windup, summoning the face of Dwight Gooden into her mind. The pitch was not destined to be a Doctor K strike, however, even though it was in the general vicinity of the plate. Keith got a major piece of it. The ball rocketed out toward rightfield — Jazz territory.

Kim turned to see the ball landing in the middle of rightfield. Jazz was nowhere in sight. Kim searched and then spotted Jazz doing cartwheels out near the fence. Great, she thought, fighting an almost overwhelming urge to sit down and put her head in her hands. Finally, Julie, the second baseman, got the ball and threw it in to Kim just as Desmond crossed home plate. Now, the score was 9-1. It didn't seem possible that things could get worse.

Of course, Kim was wrong. She didn't get out of the fourth inning until Mel's scored two more runs, putting them on top, 11-1. It was not looking good for the Parrots.

At least they'd have a chance to get back a few runs now at the plate, Kim thought, as she grabbed a batting helmet. She knew she had to get a hit. She just had to. They were so far behind and time was running out. It was up to her to get something started. "Come on, Kim!" Jazz called from the dugout.

"Send it outta here!" Terry added.

Things had gotten very testy when the Parrots were out on the field. Kim was surprised that her teammates were still cheering for her. She had to admit that she hadn't been very nice to Jazz when she had been caught doing gymnastics in rightfield and Mel's got two runs out of it. But Jazz let things like that roll right off of her.

Taking her batting stance at the plate, Kim blew her bangs out of her eyes and glared at Desmond. The pitcher jammed his cap firmly down on his head and shook off his catcher's first signal. Kim gripped the bat a little more tightly and got ready. Desmond was not about to catch her napping. She was going to get a hit and get the Parrots back in the game.

Desmond went into his windup and delivered what appeared to be a smoking fastball. But Kim knew that he had a reputation for throwing first pitch change-ups. He wasn't about to get her to swing early. Suddenly, Kim realized that she was wrong and Desmond had thrown a fastball. He must have shaken off the change-up signal, Kim thought, as she desperately tried to get her bat around in time. Her weight was on her heels though, and she only managed half a swing by the time the ball thumped into the catcher's mitt.

"Strike one!" the umpire called out loudly.

Kim stepped back out of the batter's box to regroup. Swinging the bat around a few times to loosen her shoulders, she tried to ignore the instructions her teammates were calling in to her from the dugout. Knowing she was thinking too much, Kim attempted to clear her mind.

Flipping her braids behind her, Kim squared her shoulders and stepped back up to the plate, feeling a little calmer. One strike did not make an out, after all. No big deal.

When Desmond went into his windup for the next pitch, though, Kim began overthinking again. She figured that since he had opened with a fastball, he might try the change-up on this pitch. But then it occurred to her that he might want her to think that, and would deliver another fastball instead.

With a start Kim suddenly realized the ball was heading toward her and she was not ready. She barely had enough time to shift her weight to her front foot before the ball whizzed past her. It registered in her mind that Desmond had thrown another fastball just as the umpire called out her second strike.

"Kim, pay attention!" Breezy yelled from the dugout.

Kim gritted her teeth and tried to do what Breezy instructed. Instead, her mind kept wandering back to her pitching fiasco. Then she started worrying about the next inning. She didn't think she could handle the humiliation and embarrassment for even one more pitch. Kim wondered why somebody else on the team couldn't pitch. At this rate, she'd end up on the local news's lowlight films with all the other sports bloopers and mishaps. Not exactly the preferred road to fame.

Once again Kim was brought back to her present precarious position as the ball left Desmond's hand. This time she registered that it appeared to be another fastball and shifted her weight in plenty of time. As her bat came around in a quick, even swing, Kim's heart sank. She realized that Desmond had duped her with his shiftiest change-up, and the pitch hadn't been rocketing toward the plate — it was traveling at more of a stroll. Desperately trying to slow her bat, Kim knew it was all over. She didn't even need to hear the umpire's call to know that she had struck out.

Kim walked slowly back to the dugout in disgust. She threw her bat and helmet on the ground and then dropped down on the end of the bench.

"What were you doing?" Breezy practically exploded, as she crutched over to Kim. "You obviously didn't have your mind on what you were doing at all. You should have just called in your swings from the dugout, because you weren't even there. Get your head into this, Kim. We can't win without some effort from you."

"Come on, Terry!" Ro called out from the edge of the dugout, forcing Kim's attention back to the field.

Kim saw that Terry was already in the batter's box, swinging her bat ferociously and glaring at Desmond. She bit her lip, and couldn't think of anything to say to Breezy. For some absurd reason she felt like laughing. She had a picture of herself in her mind, sitting in the dugout with a bullhorn. Every time Desmond pitched, she'd call her swings out loudly. Fighting to keep a smile off her face, Kim knew that Breezy would not appreciate the joke at all — even if it was hers to begin with.

Kim was well aware that this game had become a major blowout and embarrassment for the Parrots and she should take it more seriously. But something about pressure and stressful situations brought out the worst in Kim's sense of humor. Jokes ran through her head even though it was not a good time to share them with anyone. Kim guessed that Breezy was right when she said humor and baseball didn't always mix.

Besides, Breezy did have a point. Kim's mind had not been on her batting. She thought too much at the plate and didn't even focus on the pitches. Kim knew better. But, she just couldn't seem to concentrate today. Kim yawned and swung her feet. She was really, really tired.

"Strike three!" the umpire called, bringing Kim back to the present. Startled, she blinked as Terry stalked back to the dugout with a big frown on her face. Kim couldn't believe she had missed all of Terry's at-bat. Where was her mind?

"I kept expecting his change-up," Terry said angrily, plopping down next to Kim. "Instead, he just hit me with fastballs. It's the not knowing that did me in. I can't believe it."

"I don't believe you, Terry," Breezy retorted. "How could you not have gotten a piece of *anything* out there?"

"Listen, Breezy, just because you can't get up there and take your turn at bat doesn't give you the right to jump all over us," Terry said angrily, her green eyes blazing. "It's a lot easier to say than do, you know."

"Don't tell me what I can do," Breezy snapped. "I know I could get a hit off this kid. He doesn't throw the change-up all that often anyway."

"An average of 2.7 times an inning," Crystal piped up, sounding surprised that she had spoken.

"See?" Breezy asked triumphantly. "So what's wrong with you guys?"

"Breeze," Kim began, cutting Terry off before she

could retort, "you know it's the threat that's the problem. You don't know when he's going to throw it, and it keeps you off balance."

Suddenly, Kim had an image in her mind of each of the Parrots tipping and toppling over at the plate because they were so off balance. A short giggle escaped before she could stop herself.

Breezy spun around and glared at her. "I don't see what's so funny here, Kim," she practically spat out. "We're getting slaughtered and the Parrots are going to be the laughingstock of Emblem."

Feeling really tired, Kim could only stare at her cleats and nod. Breezy was right, of course. There was nothing funny about this situation. But Kim didn't know what else to do but laugh at the game — it was that bad.

Sarah popped out to the shortstop and the inning was over. Kim sighed, picked up her glove, and slowly headed out to the pitcher's mound without looking at Breezy. Kim was suddenly hungry and wished she had gotten a last meal, like prisoners get before heading for their executions. Because that's exactly how she felt, as if she was heading for her own execution.

It was as if an endless inning stretched out before her. Kim didn't know how she was going to face it — without giving in to her sense of the absurd. And then, she had no idea how she would face Breezy.

"Oscar, I don't know about this," Kim said, rocking back on her heels and peering down at the wire cage in front of her. It was Sunday afternoon and the two of them were in the Yardleys' family room. "I feel kind of bad for these mice. I mean, maybe they don't really want us to make them famous as part of our behavioral study."

"Of course they do," Oscar countered, pushing a lock of red hair out of his eyes and staring at Kim over the tops of his glasses. "I mean, this is an opportunity for them to really contribute to society instead of running around some dumb wheel over and over again. We're giving them the chance to make their own individual mark on humanity."

"O, you're beginning to sound like Dr. Frankenstein, or something, or that old dude who died before he could give Johnny Depp hands," Kim said with a grin, elbowing Oscar in the ribs playfully. "You know, the guy in the movie, *Edward Scissorhands*."

"Kim, we're talking mice here," Oscar reminded her,

gesturing to the three cages in front of them. "We're not talking about genetic reconstruction, you know."

"Well, maybe I just don't like to see living things in cages," Kim said. "I think we should set all these mice free when we're done with them and give them a new lease on life."

"Yardley, you sound like a commercial for a vitamin or something," Oscar kidded her, reaching into one of the cages and taking out a small white mouse.

"Geesh!" Kim exclaimed. "All of these dudes look alike, you know. How in the world are we going to tell them apart? How do we even know who's male and who's female?"

"Ye of little faith," Oscar responded solemnly. "First of all, they shouldn't get mixed up because each group of four has its own cage. Second of all, we'll tag them so if they do get mixed up, we know which group is which."

"Hmmm," Kim said. "Good idea. But how do we tag them? We can't exactly sew name tags into their fur, you know."

"No, but we can tape different colored bands around their legs," Oscar suggested.

"Bingo," Kim agreed. "You are a genius, Oscar Slaughterbeck. A true genius."

Oscar blushed and put the mouse he was holding back into its cage. "So, what do we use for tags?" he mused, looking around the family room for inspiration.

"You're it!" Josh screamed suddenly, running into the

family room with Jenny right behind him.

"No, you're it!" Jenny screamed.

"Speaking of tag," Kim said to Oscar with a grin.

"Very funny, Kim," Oscar replied.

"Leave me alone!" Jenny yelled. "You're hurting."

"You're a baby!" Josh admonished his sister with a frown. "Cry baby! Cry baby!"

"Kim, make him stop!" Jenny yelled, coming over to Kim and putting her arms around her waist.

"No problem, buddy," Kim said. "Stop, J-Man! And leave the kid alone, ho-kay?"

"Hey, what's that?" Jenny asked, looking at the cages on the floor.

"Yeah, what's that?" Josh asked with interest, coming over to stand next to his twin sister.

"Mice," Oscar replied.

"Oooh, can we play with them, too?" Jenny crooned. "Puh-leaze, Kim. Puh-leaze!"

"No, they're for school," Kim said. "Only Oscar and I can play with them. So, why don't you two go —"

"Kim, I'm leaving for the airport in a little while," Mr. Yardley said, walking into the room wearing a clean light-blue button-down shirt, tan pants, and a brown blazer. "And I wanted to make sure you had everything in order for Mom's big welcome home."

"Ooooohh, Dad, don't you look spiffy," Kim commented with a smile at her father.

"Thanks," he replied. "So, I'll see you in a few hours.

I'll call if the plane's going to be late."

"Okay, Dad, and don't worry about a thing," Kim said. "I've got it all under control."

An hour later, Kim wasn't so sure. Twelve mice and two screaming 6-year-olds, plus Richard's blaring Guns 'n Roses music, and Faith's less than enthusiastic reception of the poor little creatures had given Kim a pounding headache. She and Oscar were down in the basement because Faith had had such a fit about the mice. Kim knew Faith could scream, but she'd never heard anything like these screams. Richard was right. The girl had a future in horror movies, with a bloodcurdling scream like that.

"So, O, it's been a day and a half, hasn't it?" Kim asked, turning to Oscar. "I hope these guys will be okay down here. I still don't understand why Faith had such a fit about keeping them in our room, you know. They're probably safer from Ninja down here, though. That cat looked like she would love to get her paws on one of our subjects."

"That's true," Oscar agreed. "You know how females are. Now, let's go over who's who again," he said, surveying their handiwork.

"Yes, Boss," Kim replied. "Mice in cage with Hulk Hogan stickers and yellow tags get food pellets whenever they hit the bar. Mice in cage with green soccer ball stickers and green tags get food only sometimes when they hit the bar. And finally, dum-dum-de-da . . ."

Kim paused, looking over at Oscar dramatically.

"Kii-iih-iim!" she heard Jenny yell. "Pho-one. Breezy."

"Hey, Kim," Josh added. "Can we come down? I want to see the mice. Please?!"

"Oh, no, O!" Kim exclaimed. "I forgot I was supposed to go to Breezy's for a post-game talk. How could I have forgotten? Not that I really need to hear anyone tell me how badly I pitched yesterday. We were slaughtered. There's not much else to say."

"Kih-ih-immm!" Faith yelled. "Phone. Hurry, I need to make a call."

"Well, O, I guess I better go," Kim said. "We've got everything set up so we can start evaluating Operation Mice next week, right? So, whichever group hits the bar the most is the lucky winner of . . . a trip for four to Mickey Mouse's house in sunny Orlando, Florida," she concluded, imitating a game show announcer's voice.

"You're clearly going over the edge, Yardley." Oscar replied. "I don't think mice do well in hot climates. But, I could be wrong. I should probably get home anyway."

Kim and Oscar laughed and then checked that the three cages were all closed securely. Kim flipped off the light and the two kids bounded up the stairs.

"Breeze," Kim said breathlessly into the receiver as soon as she picked up the phone. "What's up?"

"Where have you been?" Breezy asked angrily. "I've been waiting for you to show up all afternoon."

"I'm on my way over," Kim said, ignoring her head-ache and the overwhelming feeling of exhaustion that seemed to be taking over her body. "Be there in a few."

"See you," Breezy replied shortly and then hung up the phone.

"Good conversation?" Oscar commented, coming around the corner.

"The best," Kim agreed. "Well, I better motor if I want to get there and get back before my parents come home."

"Okay," Oscar said. "Good luck with Breezy, Kim. And don't worry. You will get everything done. You're just kind of overloaded right now."

"You're telling me," Kim agreed. "See you at school tomorrow."

After Oscar left, Kim told Josh and Jenny to make sure that their rooms were neat — and stayed neat until she got back. Then she asked Richard and Faith to keep an eye on things and make sure nothing got messed up while she was at Breezy's.

As Kim sped over to Breezy's, she tried to clear her head and focus on baseball — specifically their blow-out game the day before. But instead of baseball, she found herself mulling over what Oscar had said about her being overloaded. She'd never thought about that be-fore. Maybe she had taken on too much at once. The thing was, Kim hated more than anything in the world to let anybody down. But then why did she suddenly feel as if she was letting *everybody* down?

8

"Kiiiim!" Mrs. Yardley yelled down the basement steps. "You're going to be late for school!"

Kim put the last refilled water bottle inside the last cage and closed the door. "See you later, dudes," she called to the mice. "I hope you have a relaxing day. And sorry about yesterday." With that she hurried up the steps.

"See ya, Ma," Kim called, grabbing her backpack from where she'd hung it on the back of one of the kitchen chairs and flying out the back door. She glanced down at her watch and saw that it was almost eight. She had less than 10 minutes to get to school before the bell. She started to run, her hair flying out like a cloud behind her. She'd had no time to braid it in her rush to get ready for school and check on the mice.

Those poor mice, she thought, as she ran. Actually, they were only part of the chaos that had greeted her last night when she'd gotten home from seeing Breezy. The entire house was in an uproar. She had felt bad enough after listening to Breezy telling her that she could have rallied the Parrots if only she'd focused and tried a little harder. The game against Mel's was probably their most major loss to date. But still. It was easy for Breezy to tell her to focus. Baseball was just about Breezy's only focus in life. She didn't have to worry about science and running a family and . . . Kim made herself stop thinking like that. It wasn't fair, especially when she knew that when Breezy yelled at her, it was as if she was chewing herself out at the same time. It was just her way of trying to deal with the fact that she couldn't play baseball right now.

Anyway, as it had turned out, seeing Breezy had actually been the high point of Kim's evening compared to the disaster that awaited her when she got home. The twins had taken the three cages full of mice and brought them upstairs to the family room. They claimed the mice wanted to watch TV and didn't like it downstairs in the cold, dark basement. Where they got the idea that mice liked to watch TV, Kim had no clue. And she didn't want to know. All she knew was that she and Oscar had almost lost their entire control group.

The twins, like true freedom fighters, had chosen to liberate one group from their cage and let them run around. By the time Kim walked through the door, Ninja was chasing them all over the house. Red was barking, Richard was playing M.C. Hammer's "U Can't Touch This" at top volume, and Faith was nowhere to be found. The twins, of course, were just standing there as if they had no idea how any of this had happened.

In the midst of this melee, her parents had arrived home from the airport. It was quite a scene. All the cushions were off the couch, chairs were turned over, and drawers pulled out, as a result of the effort to find the mice. Eventually, her mother and father had been the ones to rescue the mice, which made Kim very happy. The lecture she got afterward about being the oldest and living up to responsibilities was not so great, however.

And now, here she was, running to school because she was late. She felt more scattered than she had before — if that was possible — and it was only Monday morning.

She flew up the school steps just as the final bell rang. Then she tore up the stairs to the second floor to dump her books in her locker and get her math notebook, since she had math first period. Some kids were still in the hall, so it looked like she was going to make it on time.

"Hey, Yardley," someone called out. "You ready for the quiz?"

Kim turned just as Jimmy Hsu walked up beside her. "Quiz?" Kim asked, her stomach starting to do flip-flops. She hadn't studied for any quiz. How could they be having a quiz that she didn't know about? She always studied for quizzes and she always did well — especially in math and science.

"Yeah, you know, the quiz on negative integers," Jimmy said, looking at her as if she was crazy. "I know Mel's kind of whipped you on Saturday, but still."

"Oh, no," Kim groaned. "I totally forgot about the quiz. And Jimmy, please don't mention that game. As far as I'm concerned, it's ancient history."

"Just ranking on you, kid," Jimmy said as they entered the classroom. "I've seen your arm. I know you're awesome. You were just hiding it well on Saturday."

"Good luck on the quiz," Kim said, trying to smile but not exactly succeeding.

"Yeah, you too," Jimmy replied, walking toward the front of the room.

Kim slowly slid into a seat in the back row and put her head in her hands. She could not believe how terribly this day was going. How could she have forgotten about a math quiz? Where was her mind? Breezy was right; she really did have a focusing problem, and it wasn't just baseball either.

Kim didn't know how she made it through the rest of the morning. She brought the wrong book to English so she couldn't answer any questions and then totally blanked in science when Mr. Krasnow asked her to explain the frog's digestive system, something she knew like the back of her hand.

By the time lunch rolled around, Kim was ready to pack it all in and call it a day. But as she dumped her books into her locker, she figured things had to get better. They couldn't get worse. Could they? Just then Kim spotted Breezy leaning on one crutch while trying to put some of her books in her locker. Kim knew she ought to go talk to Breezy, but she just wasn't interested in going over all the horrible details of the blow-out game again. She felt so tired and scattered at the moment, it was hard to think of what to say to get the conversation off to a good start.

"Hey, Breeze, want some help?" Kim asked, as soon as she reached Breezy's locker. She figured that was a good opening. Not too pushy, not too cheery. Basically just friendly. Maybe Breezy had calmed down and they could act as if the game hadn't even happened. It felt like a bad dream to Kim anyway.

"I've got it," Breezy replied curtly.

"Breeze, about being late yesterday —" Kim began, kicking her green high top against the floor.

"Kim," Breezy interrupted, cutting her friend off abruptly. "Forget it, okay. I don't want to talk about it anymore. You obviously didn't think a post-game talk was as important as I did. It's pretty clear."

"But you don't even know what happened," Kim protested, frowning. Kim's attempt at good humor was fading fast.

"Well, please enlighten me," Breezy retorted, turning back to her locker.

"Hey, Red," a guy's voice called out. "What's up?"

Just then Jace Jeffries walked over to where the two girls were standing. Breezy looked at him with a stony face and Kim smiled stiffly, wondering what in the world he wanted with her.

"So, Red, how about you and me being partners for the dance contest?" Jace asked smoothly, running a hand through his hair and staring at Kim with those amazing grey-blue eyes.

"Uh, sure," Kim replied without thinking. All she wanted was for him to leave them alone so she could finish her conversation with Breezy and try to get things back to normal.

"How about if I pick you up at seven on Friday night?" Jace continued in the same smooth voice. "I bet the two of us will blow them all away with our skill on the floor. I hear you're great. We'll have this contest thing in the bag, no problem."

Kim just stood there, smiling dumbly at him while still very conscious of stone-faced Breezy standing next to her.

"Well, see you around," Jace concluded, before turning and taking off down the hall.

"Breezy," Kim began, taking a deep breath. "You know I —"

"Kim, I don't need to hear anymore," Breezy retorted angrily. "You obviously care more about some stupid dance contest than about the Parrots. I get the picture. You don't have to fill it in for me. And hey, don't do me any favors. I didn't really want to get together with you yesterday either."

"Breezy, listen —" Kim began. What Breezy was saying was totally untrue. The Pink Parrots were one of the most important things to her. Didn't Breezy know that? That would never change, no matter what.

"Save it, Kim," Breezy interrupted. "And forget about being captain. As far as I'm concerned, it's just not working out."

With that, Breezy turned and stormed away down the hall on her crutches.

Kim bit her lip, trying not to cry. In all the years they'd been friends, Breezy had never said anything so mean. She hadn't given Kim a chance to explain. She felt terrible. She'd lost her best friend and a big game, plus failed a math quiz, almost killed four mice, disappointed her parents, all in two days. How was that humanly possible, especially when she'd only been trying to do the right things to make everybody happy? Now no one was happy, least of all her. Life sure got complicated in junior high — they weren't kidding.

"Hey, Yardley, how's our brood doing?" Oscar asked, walking over to where Kim still stood, slumped against Breezy's locker.

"I think okay," Kim replied softly. "I checked on them before school and they looked pretty good, even the four who got all the, shall I say, exercise, yesterday."

Oscar smiled. "Yeah, that must have been crazy," he said. "I wish I could have been there to help catch them."

"Thanks, O," Kim replied, trying to smile.

"What's with you?" Oscar asked, his green eyes staring at her intently from behind his wire-rimmed glasses.

"Where's that warped Yardley sense of humor that I know and love?"

"Kind of under wraps for the moment," Kim said. "Major fight with Breezy. Failed a math test. Definitely not my day, you know."

"Hmmm," Oscar replied. "That good, huh? What about lunch?"

"I guess," Kim answered, although the thought of food made her stomach, which was in a major knot, feel even more queasy.

"Don't sound so excited," Oscar said as the two of them started walking down the hall. "I know the cafeteria's mystery meal is nothing to write home about, but there is some nutrition hiding in there somewhere. I'm sure of it."

Neither of them said anything until they got to the double doors of the cafeteria.

"Uh . . . Kim," Oscar began before they walked inside. "How would you . . . um . . . like to . . . uh . . . be my partner in the dance contest?" he finally blurted out in a rush.

"Um, I'd . . . um . . . love to," Kim replied, pushing the doors of the cafeteria open and walking toward the lunch line.

"Great!" Oscar replied happily. "When should I pick you up?"

"Um . . . I . . . uh . . ." Kim stammered, suddenly remembering she'd just told Jace she'd be *his* partner.

What was she doing saying yes to two dates for the same night for the same thing? She was really losing it, no doubt about it.

"What did you say, Kim?" Oscar asked, putting a carton of milk on his tray and turning to her.

"I love corned beef hash, don't you?" Kim countered, grabbing a heaping plateful. Actually, she hated corned beef hash with a passion, but she had to say something to change the subject.

"You do?" Oscar asked. "I didn't think anybody could love something that looks like dog throw-up, sorry to be so gross."

Kim just looked at him and nodded without saying anything. At least she'd gotten Oscar off the subject of the dance contest. The thing was, what in the world had she gotten herself into? And how was she going to get herself out of it without hurting anybody's feelings?

She just couldn't say no. First, she'd overloaded with responsibilities at home, at school, and on the baseball field, and now she'd overloaded on partners for the dance contest. As Kim followed Oscar to the end of the lunch line, she started thinking that she had, without even trying, gotten herself into a major mess. She was only trying to do the right thing. How could the right thing have suddenly turned out to be so wrong?

9

Kim did not know how she made it through the rest of the week. It helped that she hadn't in fact failed her math quiz, but she had gotten a C. For her, a C was almost an F because she usually got A's. Baseball practice had been torture, too. Breezy still wasn't really speaking to her, and Kim could not believe that she had to pitch again tomorrow against Mitchell Lumber.

"Kim, are you ever coming out of there?" Faith whined from the other side of the bathroom door. "You've been in there forever and I'm going to be late to Jeannie's slumber party all because of you."

Kim looked at her reflection in the mirror. Forever had been more like six or seven minutes, but exaggeration was basically Faith's only form of expression. Kim was used to it. She fixed one of her braids and sighed, in no mood to hurry. She could not believe how much she did not feel like going to this dance now that she had two dates. She wished she had no dates. Why had she ever said yes to Jace in the first place? Kim thought Jazz was probably more excited about Kim's date with gorgeous Jace than she was. Kim wished Jazz could take her place, but Jazz was going with Desmond. She'd asked him herself. That was one thing Kim had to admire about Jazz — she went after what she wanted and got it most of the time.

"Ki-ih-im! Come on!" Faith yelled, banging on the door.

"Hold your horses," Kim said. "I'm coming."

She opened the door and walked out of the bathroom, tucking her blue T-shirt farther into her long blue and white striped shorts.

"You're wearing *that* to a dance?" Faith squealed. "Kim, you look like you're going out to play baseball, or something."

"I'm comfortable," Kim replied defensively. "I dance better this way. I can't feel restricted."

"I guess," Faith said. "But high-top sneakers? Don't you think that's taking it a bit too far?"

"Hey, Faith, whatever floats your boat, you know what I mean?" Kim retorted before turning and walking down the stairs. Usually so patient, Kim felt completely on edge.

As soon as the doorbell rang, Kim opened the door. "See you later," she called out in the direction of the family room before anyone could get to the door in time to check out Jace. She didn't feel like explaining anything about him, especially since she didn't know why she was going with him in the first place. Oscar would be so hurt if he ever found out he was one of her *two* dates to the dance. She'd just have to make sure that it didn't happen, and that Jace didn't figure it out, either. It was going to be some night. There was no doubt about that.

Jace opened the car door for her and she crawled into the backseat. Heavy metal music was blaring so loudly, Kim could barely hear herself think. Jace got in beside her and then introduced her to his older brother, Jeremy, who was driving.

"I hope you're in a winning mood," Jace said loudly. "I know I am."

Kim murmured noncommittally. Dancing was the least of her worries at this point.

"So, Kim, did I tell you about the new gold stripes I'm getting on my bike?" Jace asked. "It's going to look incredibly hot."

"Hmmm," Kim said, staring out the window. She could not believe that Jace was jacking up his bike. What an incredibly geeky thing to do. Breezy would die.

Just thinking about Breezy made Kim's stomach get all knotted. She couldn't get the image of Breezy storming down the hall away from her out of her mind. Breezy had avoided her all week since then. And she'd made a point of telling the Parrots that she was boycotting the dance tonight. And that she thought they should, too, because of the game against Mitchell Lumber on Saturday. At first Kim had been mad, but now she was just sad. She realized that the truth was that she missed hanging out with her best friend — a lot.

Before Kim knew it, they had pulled up in front of the school. Jeremy was so into the music on his tape deck, it looked to Kim as if he'd been driving on automatic pilot. He seemed barely conscious that he had passengers. She wondered if he even knew that she and Jace had gotten out of the car. Teenagers were weird, she thought.

She followed Jace slowly up the steps and into the building. She could hear the sound of music coming from the gym. Kim had been at school at night for stuff before, and it always made her feel strange — kind of like they must be breaking rules, even though she knew it was all totally legit.

"Aren't you psyched?" Jace asked, turning to her with a grin.

Kim just gulped and smiled weakly. Actually, she had to make sure she and Jace didn't walk into the gym together since she had told Oscar she had stuff to do at home and would meet him at the dance. She hated lying to him, but it had really seemed like the only way.

"Uh, Jace, I . . . uh . . . I . . . have to uh . . ." Kim stammered, trying to think of a way to get away from him for a minute without making it seem suspicious.

"Kim! Hey, Kim!" a voice suddenly yelled.

Kim froze in place, terrified that she'd turn around and find herself face-to-face with Oscar. She stood rooted to the spot like a statue.

"Kim, wait up!" the voice repeated, as Jazz came into view running down the hall.

How she could have thought for even a moment that Jazz's voice was anything like Oscar's was totally beyond her, but it definitely showed how paranoid she was. What a night it was going to be!

"Isn't that one of your girlfriends?" Jace asked, eyeing Jazz appreciatively as she approached them.

"Yeah," Kim said quickly, still racking her brains for a way to get away from Jace before Oscar showed up. Kim had to admit that Jazz looked great, as usual. She was wearing a short cropped white denim jacket, a matching white miniskirt, and white cowboy boots. She looked like one of those girls in the teen fashion magazines she read.

"Hi," Jazz gushed at the two of them. "I'm soooo excited about this dance, aren't you?" she continued, batting her eyelashes at Jace, who smiled back.

Kim didn't give a hoot that Jazz was flirting with her date. She just needed a way to get away from the both of them before Oscar got there.

"Yo, O!" Kim suddenly heard a deep male voice boom. She didn't have to turn around to know that it was Hector Martinez. He was the biggest kid in Emblem, and had the deepest voice of any kid in their school. He was also friends with Oscar. Kim had to get out of there — fast.

"I'll meet you in there," Kim blurted out and turned

and took off down the hall before Jace or Jazz could say anything. She rounded the corner fast and bumped into Terry, who had just walked in with Iceman, a pitcher for Quicky Chicken.

"Hey, Kim," Terry said loudly.

Kim looked frantically at her, put her finger to her lips, and continued running down the hall. She knew Terry and Iceman probably both thought she had lost her mind, but she had no choice. She was determined that Oscar not know that she'd come here with Jace.

Just then she noticed the girls' bathroom on her right, so she ducked inside. She staggered over to one of the sinks and leaned against it. She had to think. The dance hadn't even started and she was already out of control. Definitely a bad sign. She bent down and turned on the tap and splashed her face with cold water. Then she grabbed a paper towel and started scrubbing it dry.

Just then the bathroom door burst open and Lindsay Cunningham sauntered in, followed by her loyal band of followers, including Gwen, Beth, and Tory Hibbs, Kim's favorite.

"Sweet outfit for a tomboy," Lindsay said obnoxiously, eyeing Kim up and down, the distaste obvious on her face. "You baseball girls know about as much about fashion as Joe DiMaggio."

"Well, I guess we can't all look like triple scoop strawberry ice cream cones," Kim retorted. "And, Lindsay, just for your information: Joe DiMaggio hasn't played baseball for a long time. You might want to get with the program, you know."

"You're just jealous," Tory Hibbs began.

"Jealous of an ice cream cone?" Kim asked snidely.

"You wish," Lindsay shot back. "Anyway, Kim, good luck in the dance contest. We know you'll need it if you dance anything like you pitch."

Kim balled her hands into fists at her sides, glared at Lindsay and her clones, and stalked out of the bathroom. She hurried toward the gym, still mad at Lindsay. She could not believe she had actually wasted her time talking with her, let alone getting into something of a fight. She never usually paid them any attention or let them get to her. Where was her good old Yardley sense of humor? It seemed to have disappeared, along with her easygoing personality.

Kim peered into the gym, trying to scope out who was where. It was sort of hard to tell since the lights had been dimmed a little to create "atmosphere" and there were some pulsing strobes flashing on and off. Kim edged along the wall, her eyes darting back and forth. She felt like she was walking through a mine field, as if each step was bringing her closer and closer to possible death. The terrors of dating, Kim groaned inwardly. She could not wait until this night was all over.

"Kim, where've you been?" Oscar asked suddenly, as he walked up to where she was standing against the wall in the shadows.

"Uh, here and there, you know," Kim answered quickly.

"So, how's everything going with the mice?" Oscar asked with a grin. "Have they gone on any excursions around your house lately?"

Kim just smiled halfheartedly, her eyes still scanning the gym. She just did not have it in her to give Oscar one of her usual comebacks. All she could do was worry that Jace would appear out of nowhere and Oscar would find out the truth.

"Is everything okay, Kim?" Oscar asked, the concern evident in his voice. "You seem a little preoccupied."

"Me?" Kim responded, trying to sound surprised. "I'm having a great time," she added in as light a tone as she could manage. Even she could tell, however, that her light tone sounded mighty heavy and solemn.

"Kim, there you are!" Jazz squealed, coming up to where Kim and Oscar were standing. "I am having the best, best time. Desmond is the *best* dancer. He could like go on *Party Machine*, you know that show with all the dancing? I told you he would be a great dancer. I could tell just from watching the way he moved when he was pitching."

"Jazz, that's very interesting," Oscar said. "I never realized that playing baseball and dancing were so closely related and that the skills for one would carry over to the other."

"So, Kim," Jazz began, "where's —"

"I have to go get something to drink," Kim said quickly, cutting Jazz off. "I'm totally parched."

Jazz and Oscar both looked at her as if she was crazy.

"See you guys, later," Kim said. With that, she took off across the room toward the refreshment table. She grabbed a paper cup of punch and leaned against the table for a minute, trying to figure out what to do next.

"Kim, I've been looking all over for you," Jace exclaimed, walking over to her. "We ought to dance so we can get our routine together for the contest."

Routine, Kim thought frantically to herself. She did not like that word one single bit. Dancing was probably the last thing in the world she felt like doing. And she had the feeling that dancing with Jace was going to be very different from dancing with Richard.

Before she could really respond, Jace grabbed her hand and pulled her out onto the dance floor. Kim felt like she was caught in a nightmare, with no choice but to be pulled along, just hoping she'd wake up soon and realize that the whole thing had never happened. The dance floor was packed with kids. Kim figured that was good. She might get lost in the crowd and Oscar wouldn't see her.

Jace started dancing quickly, moving his feet around a lot and shaking his arms. She wished he would slow down a little — the beat was definitely not that fast. Kim tried to keep up with him, but she felt totally offbeat. It was pretty obvious that Jace had no rhythm.

She didn't know how she made it through the song, but it finally ended. She told Jace she wanted to sit the next one out. He looked like he was getting a little frustrated with her, but he followed her over to the corner of the room. The two of them stood there for a few minutes, not saying anything. Kim really wanted to get away from Jace before Oscar saw the two of them together, but she didn't know how to do it without making him totally mad. She already knew that he thought she was acting weird. And she *was* acting weird.

"Hey, Kim," Terry boomed loudly, as she walked up to where Kim and Jace were standing. "Oscar's been looking all over —"

"Uh, hi, Terry," Kim cut her friend off. "Do you know Jace? Jace, Terry. Terry, Jace."

"Terry," a breathy voice called. It was Jazz, who was walking over to them. "Have you seen Kim? Oscar's looking for her."

"Who's this Oscar kid?" Jace asked suspiciously. "And why's he looking for you, Kim?"

"Ummm . . ." Kim began helplessly. She felt like a cornered animal.

"There she is, Oscar," Crystal's voice announced happily. "I knew she was here somewhere."

This is not really happening, Kim thought helplessly as five pairs of eyes stared at her. Her life was about to end — all because she'd said yes to too many people. She felt terrible that she hadn't confided in her friends, who might have been able to help her out. She hadn't been able to tell Breezy since she wasn't talking to her, and somehow it had never come up with Jazz or Terry or Crystal since they were all excited about her date with gorgeous Jace.

"Kim, where've you been?" Oscar began, walking up to her with Crystal. "Oh, hi," he continued, looking around at all the other people.

"Who is this guy?" Jace asked obnoxiously, flipping his hair out of his eyes.

"Who are *you*?" Oscar retorted, pushing his glasses up on his nose and pulling himself up to his full height, which was still about six inches shorter than Jace.

"I'm Jace Jeffries," Jace said, glaring at Oscar. "And if you don't mind, Kim and I have to get back to the dance floor to perfect our moves for this contest." *He* had to perfect his moves, Kim thought, that was for sure.

He pulled on Kim's arm, but she just stood there rooted to the spot.

"I thought you were my . . ." Oscar began, and then let his voice trail off. Before Kim or anybody could say another word, he took off across the gym.

Kim didn't know what to do. Her life had turned upside down in such a short span of time that she felt as if she no longer had any control over anything.

"You were Oscar's dance partner, too?" Jazz asked, sounding confused. Terry elbowed her in the ribs and Jazz suddenly clapped her hand over her mouth.

"Hey, Red," Jace began coolly. "Nobody two-times me. So you can count yourself out as my partner." With that, he took off across the gym.

Kim slumped even lower against the wall. She felt like she was in a really bad B movie.

"Hey, don't worry, Kim," Terry said, putting her arm around Kim. "I heard him tell Joey that he had the contest in the bag with you as a partner. He obviously only cared about winning. He's a major jerk."

"He really is," echoed Jazz. "A gorgeous jerk, but still a jerk."

"Well, I deserved that," Kim said slowly. "I mean, I never should have told two people I'd go with them to the same thing. I don't care so much about Jace, but Oscar . . ." she let her voice trail off.

"I'm sure if you explain everything to Oscar, he'll understand," Crystal said softly. "He's that kind of person."

"I hope so," Kim agreed. "Well, guys, I think this is my cue to exit. I'll see y'all tomorrow at the game. Okay?"

"You sure you're okay, Shorty?" Terry asked.

"Yeah, yeah," Kim responded. "I just need a little time to think and to put stuff in order — especially before the game tomorrow."

She waved good-bye to her friends and walked quickly out of the gym. She *did* need time to think, but she hadn't told her friends what she really had to do. Suddenly, it was all very clear. And she'd talk to Oscar tomorrow and tell him the truth, too. There was just something even more important that she had to deal with first. She'd finally learned her lesson — the hard way. Never again would she say "yes" to everyone just because she felt like she had to. Part of life was making choices and being realistic about what was possible. She'd never make that mistake again. It was too costly.

Kim picked up her pace as she walked the last block. She knew it was now or never. Kim walked up the front steps of the white house with the green shutters that she knew so well. She rang the bell, tapping her feet impatiently. Suddenly, she couldn't wait another second.

Finally, Kim heard someone coming. She held her breath as the door opened. Breezy was standing there, leaning on her crutches.

"Kim, what are you doing here?" Breezy asked in surprise. "I thought you were going to the dance. It isn't over yet, is it? Did you win?"

"No," Kim replied quickly. "I left a little early. I was wondering if maybe we could go over the sidearm fastball one more time, you know before the game tomorrow?" Kim blurted out her words in a rush.

"Kim Yardley, you are truly warped," Breezy said with a giggle. "You want to practice pitching on a Friday night instead of going to a dance? What's with you?"

"I guess the same thing that's with you," Kim replied, smiling. "I love baseball. And I want to be focused for tomorrow."

"It's all you, Kim," Breezy said, smiling back. "You can be a great pitcher. I always said so."

"Listen, Breeze, I'm sorry —" Kim began.

"Cut it out, Kim," Breezy interrupted. "It's no big deal. I'm just mad about this stupid knee, you know. But, hey, you're here now so how about some ice cream?"

"Sounds great," Kim said. "And then I have to tell you a story you will not believe about what happened tonight. It's all about this girl who could never say no to anybody."

"Sounds interesting," Breezy said, as she led the way into the kitchen. "Especially if it has anything to do with my best friend, this girl with red hair —"

"Breeze," Kim said, cutting her friend off. "I missed you, you know."

"Me, too," Breezy agreed in a rush before changing the subject back to baseball.

Kim just smiled and patted Breezy on the back as she sat down at the kitchen table. It felt great that things were finally back to normal with her best friend. And she knew that with her extra pitching help, Kim might be able to hold her own in the game. Of course, she could always try calling her pitches in from the dugout. That might work. She'd have to ask Breezy about it later.

All she knew for sure was that she'd never be afraid of letting people down in the future; instead, she'd figure out how not to let herself down. That way, no matter what, she could always win.